GRUNGE DREAMS ON A CANVAS

LAST BOHEMIAN SUNSET RAPPELLING ACROSS THE FATE

J. SHIKHA

Copyright © J. Shikha
All Rights Reserved.

This book has been self-published with all reasonable efforts taken to make the material error-free by the author. No part of this book shall be used, reproduced in any manner whatsoever without written permission from the author, except in the case of brief quotations embodied in critical articles and reviews.

The Author of this book is solely responsible and liable for its content including but not limited to the views, representations, descriptions, statements, information, opinions and references ["Content"]. The Content of this book shall not constitute or be construed or deemed to reflect the opinion or expression of the Publisher or Editor. Neither the Publisher nor Editor endorse or approve the Content of this book or guarantee the reliability, accuracy or completeness of the Content published herein and do not make any representations or warranties of any kind, express or implied, including but not limited to the implied warranties of merchantability, fitness for a particular purpose. The Publisher and Editor shall not be liable whatsoever for any errors, omissions, whether such errors or omissions result from negligence, accident, or any other cause or claims for loss or damages of any kind, including without limitation, indirect or consequential loss or damage arising out of use, inability to use, or about the reliability, accuracy or sufficiency of the information contained in this book.

Made with ♥ on the Notion Press Platform
www.notionpress.com

Contents

Contents

Prologue

I've never been good with the endings. I've always marveled at the ability of writers to comprehend a tell-a-tale descriptive perfection of immersing the reader in a story.

As I sit abstracted at my computer screen, the cursor blinking like a ticking time bomb, I'm reminded of him, a fragmented passing memory. And before I can control the suddenness of the realization, I find myself revisiting the past, piece-wise, that almost looks continuous in the present - a predestined suffering.

Graduation (in engineering) not only ends up in good placements, bright futures and excellent packages but also rewards you with a lifetime of heartbreaks and unwanted, uninvited learnings. The curriculum might strictly adhere to engineering disciplines but the experimental explorations of emotional threadbare is more likely to turn the student into a philosopher, a poet, a psychologist, an artist, an actor, a lover and everything else that he chose not to dream of!

Pre-Lockdown

CHAPTER I

A Midnight Bustle

Aaradhya: It's 2 AM and I find myself hovering on the fourth floor of an under-construction ten-storied mall, staring at the netted iron beams rising through the cemented skeleton piercing the blackness of the midnight sky.

The JEE results were announced almost a week back and to my mother's astonishment and my horror, I found myself ranked to be competent for a seat in the shame-faced second-tier engineering colleges of India. After a day of breakdown and embarrassment of losing the subject-wise cutoff for an IIT, I decided to apply for the scholarship to attend the Undergraduate program in chemical engineering despite my coaching teacher's ardent desire and praise for a circuital branch. I've never quite understood the herd mentality that flocks people to chase a mad rush of the capitalist inclination towards software companies. It's a monopolized vogue these days to hustle the youth towards computer sciences in the name of implicit financial luxuries and trending machine learning models, anticipated to make a radicalized invention in artificial intelligence.

It breaks my heart to think that other non-circuital, core engineering branches are perceived as a rudimentary catalog of complexities that leave you unemployed at the end of the day. It is a corrupting mindset that has led to a rat race for the students, who give up on their individuality and shift control to tedious trends and societal pressure.

Monetary gains had never been the magnet of proposal for me despite the meager means of survival throughout my childhood.

Insomnia due to my nocturnal study routine has forced me to stay up today as well. I dreamily skim through the course website of my college on the second-hand, outdated version of the Lenovo laptop, reading through the syllabus contents religiously, and finding myself excited to discover familiar subjects of fluid mechanics and thermodynamics, preparing myself mentally for an elaborative discussion on them in the air-conditioned lecture halls of one of the most prestigious technical Institutes. I plug into the earphones and surf the YouTube videos, fantasizing about my soon-to-be benign college life.

I look at the frail but serene stature of my mother cocooned in a torn bedsheet, sprawled over the aberrated floor. Soon I'd be leaving her. *Leaving her.....* I drive the thought away, abashed at the desire to hurt her with yet another tragedy.

Life has been haphazard since Papa's demise two years back. Most of our family had cut us off at the prospect of my education. It might be the 21st century for the rapidly advanced digital globe, but back in the rural suburbs, female education is still a cultivated myth and doomed a curse for most villagers in the deserts of Rajasthan.

The moon shines slyly at the poverty-stricken face of my mother, ridiculing the wrinkles of toil and turmoil. I lie beside her, burying my arm in the hollow of her shrunken belly, observing the rhythmic rise and fall of her chest as she breathes heavily. I see a red velvet mite scuttling on the floor, next to her pillow and my eyes brim with tears at a distant memory. It's a July dusk of a torrential downpour, I'm seated on the floor of a newly constructed duplex, absorbed in the McMurry and Fay of organic chemistry and my father sits at a distance, finishing the furnishing of the window sills. I look up at his sound of amazement, "Aaradhya, come over here look, a sawan ki token - just like you". I walk over irritated at being disturbed, my father holds out his hand and gently places the red velvet mite onto the palm of my hand and it begins to crawl shyly. "Wow! What is this?"

"Sawan ki tokri" he repeats, his voice beaming at the discovery. "It's an insect of grace, flourishes only during the monsoons hence the name sawan ki tokri. We grew up collecting and placing them in paper baskets as kids. It's a miracle that I found one crawling on the window here." I carried the perishable creature and placed it in my geometry box, watching it snuggle next to the eraser. The next day, I aced my practice test and have been biased to think of the red mite as some sort of a lucky charm ever since.

I wake up to the clanking sounds of my mother washing the utensils. I get out of bed and sleep groggy and sullen, my mother decidedly pours an instruction manual for the day ".....curd is in a bowl of the atta container, chapatis have been placed in the white cotton cloth, eat as much tinde ki sabzi as you can and keep the rest under the stove and I'll be back early."

I am too irritated and cut her curtly with a "Hmm" and a perfunctory nod. She wraps her arms around me and kisses my cheek.

"Deep will be here by afternoon and I need you to feed him well and tell him that you cooked the meals yourself."

"No. I will do no such thing" I speak in a distasteful irritation. "Why do you have to get him involved Ma? You know I'm not a child anymore. I can get my documents verified and find my hostel. The college campus is a safe place and I'm more educated than he ever will be."

"Shhh. That's not what you say about your cousin's brother. You might be more educated academically, but he will always harbor more manly wisdom. He's going to be your protection and shelter darling. You need to be more respectful and obedient."

I quit arguing with her. Later that morning, I felt a little troubled watching her leave to take tuition in the rainy weather. Ever since Papa's death, I've seen her struggle to sustain my education and provide ourselves with two square meals a day. I immediately regret my ungrateful and impolite tone. Papa was a daily wage construction laborer and my mom assisted him now and then despite being humbly educated. She decided to take up private tuition to assist us economically after he died. We've never stayed in one house for long enough. Most of my childhood was marred by the instability of change. Whatever building father was working in used to become our temporary lodging. The only materialistic constants were a stove, a couple of utensils, 2 buckets, a few tattered sheets, and a large carton full of my books. Despite all the hurdles, my mother was always biased to believe that I was a deeply sensitive but prodigious child. I grew up at the expenses, scholarships, and mercy of my missionary school where the nuns, the teachers, and the girl student population of 1k became increasingly fond of me. Nobody in my familial lineage had ever managed to study beyond 8th grade except my mother who fought vehemently to continue finishing her BA graduation in English literature. She was then forced to marry my illiterate father with one acre of land in Bikaner which was snatched away soon by my shrewd relatives and we were turned out when my mother voiced out her concerns for my education. We shifted to the city of Jodhpur when I was three and my personal story hence stemmed.

The July clouds have lumbered across the sky, stretching like an infinite conundrum, reflecting my conflict between literature and engineering. If it weren't for my parents, I would've chased my dreams, I lie to myself like every disgruntled Indian teen. Just as I'm about to pin my hopes of my brother not arriving, I see a figure moving across the dusty road leading to our current residence. I wave at him energetically, suppressing my disappointment.

"Hi, Motu!" He greets. "You're looking more inflated than before. Almost like one of those Michelin truck tires." He makes an obtuse comment.

Oh no, no, no I tell myself, trying not to lose my composure. "How was your journey?" I divert the topic instead.

"An honorary struggle. Eager to be your chauffeur, my child."

I smile as my anger subdues. We chat for a while after eating, waiting for Mother to come back and when she does finally, Deep touches her feet. Mom smiles at Beatific with motherly affection and hugs him tight. "So good to see you Deep. Hope Aaradhya behaved herself."

"Oh yes yes maasi. Also, the food was quite nice. I missed your cooking." his voice candid with a fond longing.

We chatted for a while after dinner, discussing village politics. My mother almost cried when she heard about the unfair verdict of the Gram panchayat, owing to the land dispute concerning my mausa and maasi (Deep's parents). I pointed out that it was rather unfair of my grandfather to not allow mother and mausi a share of the maternal land. My mother reprimands me for having such audacious thoughts. I stand up angry and walk out to catch some air. I could hear Deep telling her that she was spoiling me and just because I had fared well in studies and competitive exams, it didn't give me a right to ridicule societal rules.

Tears streamed down my face as I thought about my mother's betrayal by supporting the misogynistic ideas of Deep. How could she? I thought to myself. Why can I not be opinionated just like him? Why does she hate me for the sapling that she seeded so long ago? Wasn't this the whole point of my education?

I walked by the road, trying to lose myself in the night. I climbed the footbridge and decided to stay there for some time. I took out my earphones and played Lana del Rey, watching the cars speeding below.

Happiness is a butterfly

Try to catch it every night

It escapes from my hands into the moonlight

Every day is a lullaby

The water in my eyes blurred the nightscape, until the headlights of the vehicles looked like streaks of fazed meteorite light, shooting through the blank space, lighting, expanding, burning in a continuous stream, ready to explode and burn out the blackness around it. The red and the yellow flashes surmised into an evacuated whole, imploring through the gush of nihilistic blankness that propounds the bleak human existence. I smiled at my melancholy, turning to walk back home. I almost wanted to believe that college and graduation would change my life for the better.

CHAPTER II

Remains of a rabid rage

Somewhere in the bosom of Dehradun in a light-filled 2-storeyed middle-class apartment lives a 19-year-old Siddhartha Sharma who has luckily qualified for a seat in the institute of national importance in his second attempt.

"You could've done better than chemical engineering had you studied some more. How do we show our faces to our relatives now? 98.6 percentile? And you have the fucking audacity to continue to breathe?" His father speaks in the typical baritone of mostly middle-aged, middle-class, ex-military men.

Siddhartha has hung his face low and stares at the floor as if looking hard into the whiteness of the Makrana marble would somehow miraculously brighten his fate and change his JEE rank.

"Jaane do ab" his mother tries to defend him by asking his father to let go of the matter.

"It's because of you Mira" Mr Sharma turns to direct the accusatory anger at his quivering wife. "It's because you slackened the noose around his neck and he became prey to his frivolous desires.

I can bet he loafed around with his friends, running behind girls, and masturbating 7 times a day instead of paying attention to his studies. Look where it has brought us." Mr Sharma raised his voice and rushed into the other room to bring out his leather belt.

"It's okay Sid." Mrs. Sharma tries to comfort him, incredulous at the unfolding fury in her husband. 25 years of second love marriage to Mr. Sharma has martyred the peace in her domestic life. "You will be ok as long as you don't talk back....." her voice trails off with hesitation as Mr. Gagandeep Sharma reappears, his face shining with a ruby rage.

"I will teach you an unforgettable lesson tonight. I'll ensure that you bleed tears as you go back to sleep."

Siddhartha stubbornly stares at the dusk-colored rangoli engraved on the floor, tracing the articulate outlines of the marigold-like shape, converging and diverging like a helical outlet onto itself. The metal strap of the leather belt digs into his body marking his back and forearms with blood. The floral figure seems to lift off the ground and merge into the phosphenes in his eyes as the sharp pain in his flesh travels through the thin nerve endings of the spine. Siddhartha stands obstinate, refusing to show any emotion, not even a wince escapes his stoic possession. With his shirt torn, he looks like Michelangelo's dilapidated David carved out to exude academic obscenity.

Mr. Sharma stops beating his son after about 40 minutes, gasping for breath, sweat rolling down his receding hairline. Refusing to be defeated by his son's obstinacy, he rushes into Siddhartha's room, tearing and wrecking his art and related medals and trophies. When he returns, Siddhartha is shuddering in a reflective hatred.

"You shouldn't have done that Dad. You know you shouldn't have done that. You know it's immoral."

"Oh yeah?" He slaps Sid across the face and finally surrenders the physical violence, feeling cathartic, he decides to snore to sleep like nothing happened.

Mrs Sharma sits beside him on the living room sofa, unable to look his artistic child in the eye, unable to caress his wounds. When she begins to whimper, Siddhartha turns towards her with a guilt-ridden face. "I am sorry Ma. Don't let Sejal know any of this."

Sejal is his 15-year-old sister, who is currently sleeping in her room. The stress of boards has pressurized her to lie sedimented state of a nightmarish slumber. Siddhartha walks back to his room and latches it from inside. He crawls into his closet, encumbered with stacks of overflowing coaching SMPs. He looks at them with a burning loathe. The floor is strewn with fragments of torn paintings that swirl around, forming a whirlpool ghost. A scrap of a charcoal sketch depicting a dead bird in a field of dandelions reading, (for sejal, dated 23/05/19) and signed in Sid's handwriting now lies in a corner. He hunts for the two other missing parts of the picture and finds them crumpled. He falls on his bed, dejected with despair, and tries to iron the paper and stick a cellotape to make it fall in one single frame again. *No, it doesn't look the same. It'll never look the same again. He sobs* gently.

"Bhaiya" there's a gentle tap at his door. He opens the door to let Sejal in.

"Why did you wake up? It's only 3 AM yet!"

"Couldn't sleep. I heard everything despite having my head buried in the pillows."

"Oh"

"I'm sorry. I didn't come out to save you like you do. I was too scared"

"I know." He embraces her fragile frame."It's ok. It wasn't as bad as usual"

She looks at the torn shirt and iodine bruises spreading like thin branches of a leafless tree across his shoulders and back. He shrugs involuntarily. "It's fine, really" he tries to lie again.

As she dresses the bruises and wipes the splattered blood, now caked dry on his hands and back she feels a familiar knot twist and turn like a knife inside her guts.

"I wanted to give you this" he hands her the painting. I thought you might like it. She held the ivory sheet in her hands, viewing her dream sketched in perfectionist strokes by his brother. She remembered telling him about a dream she had one night. She was standing in a field and the dandelions were suspended in air all around her. The ground started to turn into a swamp and she started to sink. She wanted to scream for help but her voice failed her. The dandelions started to rustle angrily. The night became blacker and just as she had sunk to her neck, she heard some music play and a raven dropped dead right beside her. At that moment she knew that the raven died to save her. The ground and the music became solid and she walked back home.

Allan Poe's poetry unfurled inside her head:

Once upon a midnight dreary

While I pondered weak and weary

Over many a quaint and curious volumes of forgotten lore - while

I nodded nearly napping, suddenly there came a tapping.....

"Thank you bhaiya" She smiled at him like he was her delicate raven, her glass god, her only religion.

"I'm sorry. He Tore it." He whimpered in a lament of the loss.

"It's still beautiful Sid. He can only gnaw and tear the paper. Not us."

The night rolled outside his window. He lay on the bed his vision along the Grey borders of the undulating Himalayas. The moon shone splattering rancid beams across the dense trees. Everything was quiet except for his struggling breath which came out in heavy whispers and sighs. Every part of his body hurt and every inch of his skin burned. His head throbbed as if on the verge of implosion, the echoes of his father's anger and hatred ricocheted through his skull, and he trembled like a fallen leaf. He knew this day would fester like an acidic memory lessening his will to live.

Every horror in his life became an undoable tangible wound. His father's words would haunt his soul and tear his heart and head for the rest of his life.

He sunk into the nightmarish mirth that neither sleep nor wake could provide an escape from.

CHAPTER III

The Displaced Misfit

After much persuasion and continuous begging, my brother has finally decided to take back half of the laddoos for himself.

"Maasi made them for you Aaru. " He says, unable to restrain the greedy twinkle in his eyes, he opens the container and the smell of desi ghee wafts in the air, tempting Deep to take it. A broad grin of satisfaction spreads across my face at the Pavlovian grasp that these ladoos hold over Deep's taste buds. "I've got to tell her to make me more." He says relishing the savoury aftertaste and helping himself with a second serving. "Keep coming home as frequently as possible. Don't indulge yourself in boys and drugs. Study hard and earn well." He throws his paternal manifestations at me and I nod in obediently "Yes Bhaiya." As Deep takes his leave, his eyes are filled with tears and he stammers, "You've done good Aaru. You've made us proud. If your Baba was here, he'd be beaming with joy."

"Thank You Bhaiya," I say with a reciprocal tenderness.

I find myself standing in a meadow made of tissue paper. *It must be 2011 and I'm in 5th grade,* looking at Harshita (my childhood best friend), waving her arms frantically in a warning. She's made of tissue paper too and as I continue to look at her, perplexed, she starts burning. Tiny flames catch her frame and blow her into an ashen soot. I try to make a move to save her but I'm stuck, I look at my hands and they are made of flesh unlike everything else. The rest of me is also as human as possible in a dream. I try screaming but no voice comes out. Soon a spark burns somewhere across the horizon, gigantic flames bursting around like fire waves. The paper world starts collapsing and burning and I find myself being encircled from all the directions. I can feel the heat pulsing through my body, everything smells like carbon and suffocation. I open my eyes with a start, sweat streaming down my face. I find myself in a room that I'm not yet acquainted with. None of the fans are working despite the switches being turned on. *Shoot! The electricity cut,* I think, becoming acutely aware of my new surroundings beginning to warp me up in the extremities of the climate of the new city. I pull out my phone from under the pillow, it's 14:37, and only an hour has passed since Deep's departure. I sit up, staring at the yet-to-be-occupied empty beds and wardrobes of my roommates. Anxiety has grappled my wake and I resist the urge to call Ma and ask if everything is okay. I try to shake off the burdensome feeling of something being wrong. *It must be because I dreamt about her, I tell* myself, unable to dilute the memories of Harshita who's been dead for 6 years now. I slide back into a resting position, trying to drift off into slumber. After a couple of restless minutes and tossing and turning in the bed, I stand up. The sudden movement injects a paralytic pain and an anemic buzz down the spine. *Fuck. Fuck.* I curse gripping the edge of the bed. I walk out of the room towards the bathroom which is thankfully on the ground floor at the extreme end of the corridor. I splash water across my face and stare at the elongated reflection in the mirror, distorted by the droplets dripping down its surface. With puffy eyes and dark circles, I look like I've been sleep-deprived for an eternity. When I come back, I find the door of the room slightly ajar and a sharp South Indian dialect bends out of the opening and hits my eardrums. I gently knock and push the door open.

"Hi." A girl around 5'9 stands before me donning a light pink tube top that hugs her twenty-four-inch waist neatly at the midriff and a black cotton skirt with Nike shoes. If I hadn't heard her speak, I would've definitely mistook her for some Indian version of Naomi Campbell. "I'm Dinisha Iyer, Electronics and Communication Engineering." She adds with an air of marked superiority. "You must be Aaradhya?" She raises her eyebrow questioningly.

"Oh umm yea, yes. Aaradhya, Chemical Engineering. " I stammer, feeling dwarfed in the presence of this *beauty with brains Diva* before me.

Dinisha shifts her gaze to a woman standing beside her. "This is my Amma" she introduces.

I gape at them, looking from one face to another, stupefied by their striking similarity in facial features and appearance. Her mother says something to her and neither of them seems willing to oblige the confusion writ large on me.

"Amma?" I blurted gawking.

"Yes. I mean my mother."

If one of them disappeared right before my eyes, I would be thoroughly convinced of time travel. These two ladies look exactly the same person just ten years apart. Her mother is wearing a blue salwar with an ankle touching white chikankari kurti. The large oxidized earrings dangling down the lobes make her look like an Indian runway model endorsing Anurag Kashyap films.

"Any idea about the others?" Dinisha waves her hands at the vacant beds.

"Sakshi Goyal, Computer Science Engineering, and Ishita Mullick, Electronics Engineering. They have not arrived yet." I answer.

Dinisha has chosen to occupy the bed next to mine. The two women start unpacking: two bottles of parachute coconut oil, dove soap bars, Surf Excel powder, loreal hair serum, and somewhere around 15 lipstick shades ranging from nutmeg nude to Irish rose to stand linearized on her study desk. Three boxes of other beauty products, body lotions, sunscreens, and moisturizers are crammed on the top shelf. Dinisha argues something about the clothes with her mother who then decides to leave three American tourister trolley bags unpacked. The overflowing clutter in her Almirah already makes it look like she is going to need more space than this. I look at the shuttered iron door of my cupboard uneasily. All I have in there is a suitcase of somewhere around 5 shirts, two pairs of jeans and two pairs of shoes. More than half of my suitcase is occupied with Kafka, Joyce, Orwell, Dylan, Hardy, Sylvia, and Dostoevsky I sneaked in without my mother's knowledge. I have been saving my pocket money to buy second-hand copies of these novels. If my mother came to know about this misdemeanor, she'd definitely disown me or perhaps worse even, kill me.

"Where can I buy buckets and some other accessories?" Dinisha asks, pulling me out of my strands of thoughts.

"No idea." I shrug.

They speak in their irritable incomprehensible language, and I strain my ears to pick up familiar words to make a sense of the conversation: *percentile, North Indian, Hindu,* and something something.... They leave the room without bothering to tell me anything.

Sakshi arrives the next day with a backpack and a suitcase. Despite being a high percentile achiever, I find her quite amicable and humble. Her extra small frame, round baby face, and 5 '1 height give her a child-like appearance suiting her frivolous disposition.

"I'll practically be a day scholar." She announces "My family lives on the outskirts of the city, but I insisted that I wanted to experience hostel life and independence."

"That's good." I appreciate her honesty as I mentally decide and rely on her continued absence. *One less in the room.*

Ishita arrives the same afternoon. She's wearing a white Levi's t-shirt and denim hotpants as she enters the room authoritatively, not caring to introduce herself or knock. "Oh no fuck that" she talks with some kind of an

Australian accent over the phone.

Direct admission of students abroad, I conclude. If I were a guy, I would spend hours daydreaming about her. Ishita is the synonym of perfection. Large almond eyes, brow touching eyelashes, well-contoured high cheekbones, and rose petal-like lips. The glasses perched on her tiny round nose give her a piercing scholarly appearance, more fit to be a medical rather than an engineering graduate.

"Guys, Ishi!" She waves delightedly in a mellifluous voice, struggling to sound as Indian as possible.

Three of us "Hey" her back in unison. After a very long minute of uncomfortable, awkward, and formal introduction about our branch and hometown, we are ensconced in complete silence, scrolling our phones.

"Anybody up for the campus and city visit?" Sakshi asks. "I could be an asset, being a localite." She grins trying to invite us.

Ishita and I decided against it and Dinisha agreed shyly.

Two days later, I found myself attending the welcome orientation program, feeling dejected, nervous, and lost, all at the same time. The hall is flooded with enthusiastic sounds of freshers, roaring whistles, and pealing waves of laughter. An ear-crashing applause reverberates after every dance and singing performance. My mission-schooled character finds it hard to smile at the obscene and unwitty stand-up comedies.

I sit agitated, nervously clutching the bag straps. I've already checked my phone for the umpteenth time in the past 5 minutes. The boy seated next to me casts a furtive glance and speaks some gibberish to his friends who then guffaw unashamedly.

Ok, this is it. I can't bear this anymore. I stand up and walk out of the hall amidst rude stares. Once I'm out on the pavilion descending the porch, I shudder, biting my lip to stop myself from crying.

My school was better. I recall with a longing. *At Least we were disciplined, all the functions used to be more informative and I used to be able to participate on stage.* Wrapped in the unpleasantness of the situation, I see Ishita storming ahead, staring past me and a boy is following close at her heels. "Ishi wait. It wasn't what it looked like."

The boys are chasing her already. There have been more than a dozen love-at-first-sight poems about her on the Instagram confession page of the college. I walk back to the room, feeling utterly misfit in the place.

I walk back to the room thinking, *only if Baba were still alive, only if I had taken up English literature at Delhi University instead of this, life would be so different......*

The next few days are marked with recruitment and interviews with the various clubs and sports teams.

After an hour of warm-up exercises for basketball, I've already decided to quit. "You're good at dribbling and passing." One of the seniors compliments encouragingly.

"Why don't you try basketing from the half-court next time? I guess you'll be a fit in the team if you make it." She continues.

I shrug, uncertain and anxious. After a couple of failed attempts at swooshing, I passed on the ball to Dinisha. *I'm not going to get any better, ever.* I can't stop thinking about my gigantic waist and sagging breasts as a source of embarrassment and restricted mobility. Dinisha is doing well and has already replaced one of the senior teammates. I trudge out of the court on the pretext of a water break. Just as I'm about to walk back, I notice a tall athletic boy in the men's section of the court, playing power forward, reminding me of Tim Duncan.

"Hot, huh?" Dinisha follows my gaze.

"I mean, good game," I say trying to sound observant instead of blushing.

"That's all, huh?"

"Yeah well.... The way that he's playing, looks like a very practiced professional. I think he is a senior."

"I'd take that as a bonus. Seniority equates to maturity."

After some more friendly matches and weary from adrenaline high and exhaustion we walk into the changing room of the sports complex. Dinisha is complaining and cursing, scratching her bruised ankle occasionally. I see the same boy standing in the queue waiting for his turn to change. He turns back and looks at me. There's something penetrative about his gaze, a depth tracing through his line of sight. I avert, trying to avoid gaping at him. The Girl's locker room has been locked so Dinisha and I leave without changing. It's already 22:07 by the time we reach the hostel gate and the warden is screaming, howling at our fickle morale and punctuality. We apologize and walk straight to the canteen. Dinisha has decided to be with her South Indian friends, leaving me alone. I nervously order a milkshake and paneer parantha and sit scrolling the mail, reading the class schedule for the first day.

None of my roommates are in the same section as mine and I'm already running late for the 8.00 AM workshop lab. After 10 frustrating minutes of figuring out the lab directions through the maze, I arrive out of breath. Even though I am 4 minutes late nobody has arrived yet. After waiting for 15 minutes I began to wonder if I was in the right place. Just as I'm about to leave, I see two students walking in, one of them is dressed in a khaki shirt and trousers. The other one is the same guy that I saw on the court the day before.

"Hi," He says in a deep and heavy voice.

"Hey? Workshop? Section-C-3?" I ask stupidly.

"Yeah!"

"We are early I suppose."

"Cool." He cuts me off curtly.

The class begins to fill up and all the 23 students of the section are already seated. There are 3 girls including me and 20 boys.

The class is already talking about the first bunk by 8.30 AM when a dashing, model-like 30-year-old person walks in. I hear the other two girls "uhffff" in lust as his perfume mixes with the air.

"Morning class. I'm Hardik Mishra and I'll be taking your labs. I'm pursuing a PhD in mechanical engineering here."

Mr. Mishra talks about lathe machine operations and instructs us to take notes. After he had finished detailing the specifications of how to work with the machine, he asked us to introduce ourselves. The students start with their name, branch, hometown, and hobbies. The guy that I've been having a crush on introduces himself as Abhimanyu Arora, CSE, from Jodhpur. "I am good at playing guitar and my friends tell me that I'm good at singing too." He adds. The class begins cooing, insisting on him to perform. I look closer, and a sudden recognition starts dawning a sense: *Oh! He's the same guy. He was in the same coaching as me.* I begin to recall. I remember seeing his name in the top five rankers in the mock tests list consistently.

"No. Not now. Let's be done with everybody's introduction first." Mr. Mishra says to Abhimanyu's relief.

"Also, I won't entertain any excuses from now on. All of you need to be wearing this Khakhi uniform for the foundry lab." He points at the guy seated next to Abhimanyu.

But that's a Taxi driver's dress, Sir, someone protests from the back and everyone starts giggling.

The two other girls are from electrical engineering and have already bonded, they leave me unnoticed.

As I'm walking for the Lecture hall, Abhimanyu jogs to join me.

"Hey, Aaradhya." He pants huskily, trying to catch my pace.

I slow down "Hi again."

"Can't speed up. Sprained my ankle yesterday."

"Oh! That's bad." I try to sound sympathetic. "Good game though," I add.

"Sorry?" He looks surprised.

"Basketball, I mean."

"Oh, yeah! Do you play too?"

"Just a rookie, noob rather. I came for the practices yesterday." I looked down embarrassed.

"What class do we have next?" He asks, diverting the topic.

"Economics"

"I feel the first-year compulsory courses are a complete sham. I mean, why bother tutoring us on something that'll barely add as a prerequisite to our stream? They should instead hold other electives."

"Yeah." I agree hesitantly. "But let's focus on the brighter side of lesser stress and more fun in the first year."

We walked in silence, crossing unkempt sports ground laden with wild grass and yellow wildflowers. The Lecture Theatre complex is a seven-storey symmetric building with a colosseum-like common entrance. The halls, tutorial rooms, and lecture classes are sequenced in a marbled perfection. We had no trouble finding our class. The circular desks with spring-supported chairs progressively rose higher at the back benches. We chose to seat ourselves at the window corner on the third last bench. The economics teacher was a short, middle-aged woman with a center partitioned hairline, her forehead prominent with a huge bindi.

Abhimanyu was already dozing off, his eyes swollen and red, struggling to keep his head up, by the time the lecturer was droning about pareto effect.

The next class was chemistry and Abhimanyu left for the hostel deciding to catch up with some sleep. I attended the next lecture half-heartedly, scribbling rough notes.

"Joined any club yet?" Sakshi asks as we are walking back from the mess.

"Nope. Not decided yet. What about you?"

"I'm planning for the robotics club, gonna be cool with all the AI stuff. If I fail, I have the eco club in mind as a backup."

"Cool. What about you Ishita?" I ask.

"Dramatics and Literary probably. Depends on what Geet suggests."

"Who's Geet?" Dinisha interjects

"Umm....my date."

"Wow, darling wow," Dinisha shouts and claps. "The hot mystery chick."

Ishita smiles shy and avoidant. "I don't want this to go around. I'm not sure about the guy yet. Also, I don't wanna ruin all the other options yet."

"Gotcha babe," Dinisha swears. "Show me the Insta profile na?" She begs.

Ishita hands her the phone with the username @Geet_full and the three of us scroll and stalk his profile. It's one of the DASA seniors in ECE. He has fair curly hair apart. His profile is jammed with him flaunting excellent dance moves, and an advertisement for Red Bull as the college ambassador.

"Cool. Very very cool." Dinisha stutters with evident envy. "I'll date him as soon as you dump him."

"Sure. Sire." Ishita says winking back at her.

CHAPTER IV

Transmissible sadness

Dronacharya Hostel is a mega monster of nine storeys. The yellow walls of the building shadow a shelter for 700 first-year students. Siddhartha's room is on the fifth floor and shares it with 3 other roommates. The window by his bedside almost reminds him of home. The mountains are posh with green vegetation and floating clouds. He sits dreamily, sketching the panoramic Vista in his sketchbook.

His roommates, Vedant Mishra (civil engineering), Deepesh Aarya(architecture), and Lakshya Nagar(computer science engineering) have already accepted him as a dork who is incapable of talking. Lakshya is the nerd, hell-bent to land as an SDE in Google. He has already mastered Python and Java which gives him an edge over his classmates. Nothing is stopping me from being the branch gold medalist. He thinks to himself as he devotes 30 minutes of his life to Saraswati and Ganesh puja every day. He is a creature of habit and meticulous routine.

Vedant has already acquired the title of mistri and majdoor by his friends for being a civil undergrad. It irks him to think that even a very laborious approach towards structural analysis and material integrity of buildings, foundry courses and industrial training would ensure a core placement of an average 6-7 LPA. His elder IITian brother has already advised him to start coding at the earliest. Vedant sleeps all day and wakes up by dusk, rolls himself a joint and sits with his laptop by around 10 PM, and pulls an all-nighter, the continuous keyboard tapping disturbs the sleep of his roommates. The clashing routine of Lakshya and Vedant has already made them sworn enemies. The silent rage and the urge to kill the other ensues like a bond of hatred between them.

Deepesh has been deeply influenced by Siddhartha's paintings and sketches and keeps bugging him every now and then, inviting criticisms and appeals for his assignments.

"You're astigmatic," Siddhartha told Deepesh as an epiphanic revelation one day. Deepesh had to Google the word to know what it meant. He refused to believe him at first but when a week later the ophthalmologist diagnosed him with astigmatism he felt shattered. A week of wearing corrective lenses has not only induced slight headaches but also repetitive thoughts:

It's a refractive error, why do I have an imperfect cornea or whatever? How do I tell Dad that the world-renowned Architect has an imperfect son? The buildings that I'll ever design shall always be aberrated with imperfections. I'm incapable of drawing straight lines. Oh God why the fuck did I insist on following my father's footsteps? Architecture is clearly not the same as drawing female nudes.

In one of his grief-stricken yet horny moments, he decided to adorn his side of the wall with naked sketches of Natalie Portman, Dua Lipa, Kate Winslet, and Anna

Hathaway.

"Mom this is un-fucking-fair." Lakshya complains to his mother like a primary school kid. "The only reason why I think I scored 29/30 in the CSP test is because the nude Hollywood actresses are positioned to face my pious Saraswati mata.....No Mom it's not because the logic in my code could've been flawed" He continues to insist, throwing a disgusted glance toward Deepesh.

"The fucking irony," Deepesh says looking at Siddhartha "is that he jerks off to these naked pictures every night, right below his pooja place and the Goddess doesn't seem to find that offensive."

"It's ok Jack Dawson" Siddhartha laughs "I think Leo would agree that your Rose looks more impressionistic than the one in Titanic."

All the first year has gone out for the local city visit. The seniors have taken it upon themselves to acquaint the freshers with the malls, art palaces, political houses, best restaurants and food stalls, city museums, and the best areas for a nature walk and trekking. Siddhartha has decided to stay back. The daily dose of depression creeps over him like an old addiction crippling his thoughts and shadowing his mind. The day has started to bleed into an inked sunset now. The crimsons of the dying dusk cast a sharp glow in the room, blazing the white walls with a sharp glow.

Grunge dreams on a canvas he writes on the top left corner of his sketchbook and starts to mix the color in his palette and the Grey sketch enlivens with hues.

"Hey guess what?" Lakshya barges into the room, beaming with excitement.

"Yeah?" Siddhartha says without looking up from his work.

"Sadhna from your branch has asked me out for a date." He continued to describe the conversation and how he felt. Siddhartha has already lost interest and connection and has retreated into his inner mind, saying Oh, wow, nice, hmm at periodic intervals.

Later that night, Siddhartha strolls on the terrace, watching the city lights unfurl beyond the fringes of the campus. His mind is muddled with chaotic throes constantly worrying him about Sejal and his mother back home. He fixates his gaze upon a distant street light flickering through the rain-drenched vapors. His Grey linen shirt clings to his body, damp from the humid sweat. A gentle breeze ruffles his hair, whooshing past his eardrums like a lullaby. Melancholy and solitude suspend over his solemn disposition.

He turns around at the sound of footsteps and soft sobs. Vedant is talking over the phone sounding very indiscreet. "You can't do this Maya. We agreed to make it work. No. No. What the fuck do you mean. No, I am not insecure. I just don't like the guy." Vedant catches Siddhartha looking at him and turns to go feeling abashed at the unintentional breach of privacy. After a few minutes, he comes back with an unlit cigarette between his teeth, his hands fumbling the depths of his pocket in search of a lighter. "Sup bro? Can I get a light?"

Extending his hand without waiting for Siddhartha to answer.

"I don't smoke."

"Oh! Well of course you don't" he casts a glance grazing his athletic stature from top to bottom "Never mind, I think I found one." He says, picking up a matchbox from under the dish antenna.

"Whatever it is, smoking is not worth it," Siddhartha speaks, sounding disappointed but concerned.

"Course not!" The smoke rises from his nose and mouth while his hand trembles a little. "And secondhand smoke is the worst. Get out of my way, you're prone to the passive smoke."

"Vedant, I don't mind smokers."

"Course not bro. And I don't smoke that much. Just occasionally."

"Sure. What's the sadness about?"

"Two years of long-distance relationship dude. It's all over now. I went to Kota for the JEE coaching and she stayed back for NEET preparation. Now that she's in a medical college, she's found someone better."

"I don't mean to suggest that the pain will recede, but I'd advise to not let it get to your head and ruin your four years ahead. You're talented Vedant."

"Yes, brother. No." His eyes brimmed and he inhaled a long puff to prevent the tears from rolling down his face. "But whatever it is that troubles you is way worse. Your sadness is almost tangible Sid. Hope it fades away too."

The night wrapped the two figures in its arms. The moonlight casts a sharp trace across their silhouettes, making a source of transmissible sadness.

CHAPTER V

The literary curse

The October evening rolled by in a cold suddenness. The mid-semesters had saddled the students with a rushing occupancy, there were some who wouldn't settle for anything less than a perfect 10.0 GPA (however impractical that might be) and the branch toppers of the first year were mostly bridging at a 9.5 pointer. Siddhartha stared at his first-year grade sheet, he had a straight A in engineering physics, and mathematics and a C in all the others landed him an average of 7.6 much to the approval of his seniors and fellow mates who congratulated him for making it above the 7.5 threshold. He knew he wouldn't be able to tell his father about the grades. His father would always lack the understanding of why his son might be able to ace the details of quantum mechanics and differential equations but not be able to solve even the simplest of Kirchoff equations. How can someone be exceptional at predicting patterns but fail to digest the simple working principles of electronic devices? His father was an electrical engineering graduate from IIT Madras and had then joined the armed forces as an officer, he'd tried hard to impose his violent ambitions on his children who had embarrassed him by taking after their mother's artistic retreats. It had been nearly 4 months since Siddhartha had talked to him at all. Silences are a confounding comfort, better than treacherous explanations and lies.

Siddhartha barely left the campus and had not adapted himself to any club or social group all these months. His evenings were religiously marked with sketching and painting and taking to Sejal, filling her with the details of his work and routine.

"How's your girlfriend?" She'd asked him one day.

"Fine." He'd yawned over the video call, sounding disinterested.

"So, that means you've got one?" She hushed and laughed.

"Yeah, nothing bizarre. I'm nineteen years old."

"Funnily, I never knew you to be the engaging type. Who is she? Someone in your branch? A music lover, perhaps? Someone opposite of what you are?" She guessed curiously.

"Ummm.....sejal, I'll call you later? I gotta jog, getting late for the practices."

"Ughhh.....you and the damned soccer..... you could give me a name and I'd suffice by stalking her profile...."

He cut the call before she could finish.

Aaradhya:

It's late and Dinisha and Sakshi are already brooding over their dreams peacefully. Ishita is on a night out with her second date. I'm rewriting the essay on "Viewing consciousness as an engineering problem". All I have managed so far is to stare unblinkingly at the blinking cursor on the monitor screen and zoning out into its blankness. I decided to retrieve the deleted folders of the previous drafts ..... The brain is an allusory model known to build itself from external signals fed into it as a dataset. If we can replicate awakening, we can create consciousness. A moment of grief or epiphany can alter your reality, which is perceptible enough to alter the future relations and courses of your actions, more like a framed wirework of complex iterations involving a multitude of sensations and emotions......

Too basic, I scolded myself. Too incomprehensible and unstructured. I couldn't do it, so I slammed the screen shut and switched off the lights. I should've gone out with Abhimanyu instead of working on something so stupid, that I hit the bed regretting every single choice I'd made.

I find myself in Jodhpur, the streets and the nightlight condense down into a familiarity, and three boys are walking in front of me. Two of them are my seniors whom I recognize by face and one of them is Abhimanyu. They are attempting to cross the highway. The rush of overloaded trucks and speeding cars is making the task herculean. The two seniors have been quick and managed without caring to notice their trailing junior who is hit by a bus in the middle of the crossing. I look at the scene horrified and before I can do anything, the accident dissolves right in front of my eyes and I realize that it was a nightmare. I am frozen in my bed staring at the black walls of the room, unable to breathe or shout. It's the second time I've had the apnea dig its teeth into my sleep in less than a week. After what seems like an eternity, I find myself moving and gasping for breath. These recurring nightmares have made it impossible for me to keep up with the morning lectures and I'm already falling behind the schedule. I fumble in the darkness and take out my notepad and pen, jotting down the gruesome details of the dream. After finishing, I text Abhimanyu

Hey! Sup?

I wait for a while, positive of him being asleep by now.

Juz chillin. Wbu?

Struggling with an essay.

Haha. Join me instead?

What's the buzz 'bout?

He sends me a 30-second video. I had to watch it twice before I could make out what it was about. It's a party at play with intensely absorbing rave music and glitching disco lights.

Ugh....I'd undergo an auditory malfunction if I came. I text him after 3 minutes.

Haha

And then he's gone.

But you good tho? I decided to not send the text. A minute later my phone rings, and the dialer displays Abhimanyu's name. I find my heart skipping a beat as I answer.

"Hey?"

"What were you typing?"

"Umm....I just had this bizarre dream about you."

"Uh-huh?" I can almost hear him smile.

"I saw you being hit by a bus in my hometown."

"Pretty graphic." He laughs. "I was hoping for a better version."

"Yeah."

After a prolonged moment of silence, he asks, "So what's the essay about and for?"

"I'm writing it for the Literary Club to be published in the college magazine."

"Read it out for me."

"Are you sure?"

"Yup"

I tell him about the essay, boring him with the words that have stopped making sense to me as I speak them nervously. I'm surprised by his attention to detail as he critiques and regards my work.

"The stuff that you read out sounds pretty Michael Crichton. Not gonna lie."

"What's that?"

"There is a video that you need to watch. I'll share the link. I guess you might find it useful. It's pretty much about - consciousness can't be created because it doesn't exist."

"But that pretty much goes against my whole idea."

"You can always build an argument against it though?"

"Yeah right."

Siddhartha is sitting on the terrace, his legs dangling down the wall. Vedant is perched next to him, stubbing the half-smoked cigarette.

"If you were to disappear any day, I wouldn't be surprised," Vedant says.

"Huh?"

"Got a pretty grim look in your eyes, like you're already gone."

Siddhartha continues to stare at the flickering streetlight below them, refusing to remark on the comment.

"Got a girlfriend yet?" Vedanta asks, refusing to give in the silence.

"Yeah."

"College?"

"Yup"

"Man, I deserve more than just one-word answers."

"She doesn't wanna make it official yet."

"Oh! Shoot! These girls....for real...." Vedant breaks into a peal of manly laughter.

"You got your stuff sorted?"

"Umm....yeah. We broke up finally."

"I'm really sorry mate."

"Never mind."

Aaradhya:

I'm standing before Aarav, a senior member of the Literary Club. He is reading my essay and when he is done, he looks up at me with a smile.

"Aaradhya, it's almost good. But we can't publish it. If you know what I mean?"

"Umm.... I'm sorry?" I ask crestfallen at the hard work being reduced to a single rejection.

"I think if you just tone yourself down a little and make your vocab a bit more comprehensible instead, I think it'd work. It's running with a lot of jargon and I'd suggest you not use a thesaurus next time." He adds, swelling with pride and authority.

"I don't use a thesaurus."

"Well, I'd say your vocab is pretty criminal just as it is. Nobody would understand it unless you make it a little neutral. People don't like taking Google breaks to decipher what a particular word might mean. It's supposed to be a fun read and not a philosophy journal publication"

He hands me back the sheet for correction.

I feel disappointed and angry at being told to rephrase the entire essay in an easy-to-understand language.

Make it Chetan-like not Joyce-like. I feel annoyed at his advice.

Chapter-6-The color ochre

The color ochre

Aaradhya:

I was in the middle of some weird dream when I heard my phone ring. Now this is the thing with music, when you hear a good one, you can barely differentiate it from reality. I thought it was a part of the dramatic monologue that my dream was building upon. After multiple rings, Dinisha asked me to answer the phone sleepily. I looked at the screen displaying an unidentified caller, and I answered.

"Hullo" An unfamiliar voice staccatoed at the other end.

"Hello?" I asked meekly.

"Aaradhya, this is Atharva."

I immediately recognized the final-year secretary of the Literary Society and straightened up, attentively.

"Umm....yes sir?"

"I've selected you and Aakash to assist as the editor for the drama script of the film club (Aagaaz) of our college. The crew is running short on members and they have multiple scripts that need some humanizing for the characters."

"Sure. Sir. I'm willing to do as you suggest."

"Cool. I need you to meet Kiran in 15 minutes in the theater hall. She'll guide you for the rest."

"Okay."

I quickly dress up and make a rush.

The stage is a giant platform rising as a facade through the earth. The pillars are decorated with intricate film straps carved out of stone, displaying the entire Film Era of India, right from the first 1913 film - Raja Harishchandra to all the other blockbusters of Guru Dutt, Shyam Benegal, Imtiaz Ali, Rohit Shetty, and others. I find myself marveling at the architecture when a guy in the same year as mine walks up from behind, shy and uncertain, and introduces himself as Aakash.

"We need to wait for the scriptwriters and Kiran ma'am." He adds

It's been nearly 20 minutes and I am almost bored with whiling away the time by binge scrolling on my phone.

"Hey!"

A girl interrupts the silence of the hall with an exuberant tone. She's wearing a blue crop top and a high-rise bootcut accentuating her perfectly hourglass figure. Her long black hair falls to her waist in splendid curls. I realize this is the kind of beauty that the artists scream about.

"Hi!" Aakash grins

The introversion of Aakash melts away at her sight and I gather that they know each other.

"You must be Aaradhya?" She looks at me ignoring Aakash.

"Yes." I nod.

"Loved your article about consciousness. I insisted Kiran ma'am that I needed you for your insights."

"Oh. Ummm.....thanks." I say Flustered.

"I'm Vanshika Aarya by the way." She introduces herself. "And the same branch as yours."

An hour later we've barely even begun discussing the script. Aakash and Vanshika argue vehemently about which of Fitzgerald's works is best. They look at me for a suspension and I admit that I prefer tender the Night over The Great Gatsby personally.

"Well, if you leave the Literary connotations aside, you'd be able to rise above your biases and be able to see that Tender is the Night is much more moving," Vanshika says, gesticulating the emphasis through her hand movements.

"It's just a story about the corrupting power of the money and is so full of the bourgeoisie lifestyle and adultery that I don't even find it relatable," Aakash says.

"Hah! And what do you find agreeable with the Gatsby? The fucking heartbreak?" Aaradhya asks annoyed.

"Yeah! Sort of......"

I see Kiran enter, and a tall boy follows her with a notepad and spectacles in his hands and a DSLR around his neck. He's wearing a round-necked white t-shirt and black joggers.

Kiran smiles at us briefly and tells us to get started with the work.

She looks stressed about something. She turns sharply and looks at the boy and mouths something. The boy looks almost tearful, there is something so poetic about his tragically sullen face that I can't help staring. He catches me looking at them and grabs Kiran's wrist, pulling her out of the hall with him. I look around to see if Aakash and Vanshika have noticed the scene but find them amusing themselves over some meme.

The sun is setting, suspending streaks of reds and purples across the greying skies. A few clouds scuttle in an aching rush. Siddhartha trudges back to the hostel room, his head hung low by the weight of the DSLR around his neck. He's still fiercely absorbed by the memory of Kiran's kiss. Her soft fragrant lips traced the contours of his mouth, grazing the corners gently with her tongue. It should've felt good. He's still waiting for the raging hormones to urge him to go back to her. But he encounters no such longing. He feels depressed, his libido shrinking by every waking moment. He suppresses the urge to tell her that he wants more than just her body. He longs for her heart and soul. He inhales sharply, hiding the stinging tears threatening to trickle down his eyes.

Aaradhya

It's early in the night. I'm weighing down the choices of food I should be indulging in for dinner. Nothing too heavy but nothing too light. The mess menu has potatoes and grams that I detest wholeheartedly. I've already scrolled through Swiggy's options but couldn't find a tongue-catching option. I open my WhatsApp messenger and there are 14 DM's 3 of which are group chats. I ignore them scroll down and halt at Abhimanyu's text.

Hey, sup?

Deciding dinner.

Join me? He texts back almost immediately.

Are you sure :')

Yeah, hurry, If you don't mind a little extra company.

Does anybody i know?

Shreya from our section.

Cool. See you in 10 at the back gate.

Yeah. Omw.

I'm waiting for them to arrive and I suddenly begin to feel imposing. What if it's their date and I've ruined it? What if he was just being courteous and I preyed upon the politeness with my unwanted presence? I try to drive away the intrusive thoughts as I see him walking towards me. He takes out the earbuds, grinning and swaying in a happy rhythm.

"She ditched us." He informs.

"Umm....oh! I'm sorry."

"What for?"

"Ruining your date night."

"No. It wasn't one. And you sorta saved me."

We walk to the nearest Cafe, I order a cup of black coffee and veg burger for myself and he orders a hazelnut frappe and falafel.

"I owe you," I say after a while.

"For?" He asks his mouth full of lettuce and hot sauce.

"Help with the essay. It got published in the magazine."

"Congrats kid!"

"It was run down a bit, almost lost its Literary essence but I'm glad it met the approval of the club members."

"An advice.... Just never lose yourself. I love the way that you can stand up for yourself and are so fiercely opinionated. "

"Ummm.....thanks." I look at him flushed, circling the burger in the sauce on my plate to avoid the blush from being observed.

We split the bill and took our leave. It's still 30 minutes before the in time of the hostel. I decide to sleep early. I lie ruminating about our time together.

I've decided to flunk lectures and edit the script instead with Aakash and Vanshika. The winter sun penetrates the morning haze, spreading its warmth along the freshly cut grass of the lawn.

I check my phone and my brows pique at Abhimanyu's text.

Bored without your company.

:(

All cool tho?

Yeah, I stuck with work.

See you in the chemistry lab.

Yup!

Cool. Baby!

We dawdle for an hour, making minor changes in the script and adding improvisations wherever needed.

It's 11.00 AM. Vedanta and Siddhartha are in the room. Vedanta is getting Stoned with Redbone playing over the speaker. The curtains of all four windows are drawn to keep out the daylight.

Too late

You wanna make it right, but now it's too late... Siddhartha vibes along, moving the paintbrush over his sketchbook in rhythmic perfection.

"It's the third week that you've stayed back from the classes." Vedanta slurs, his irises round and red.

"I'm sorta busy."

"Busy having a slow death."

The tangy air saturated with cannabis engulfs the occupants in its vapor folds.

Aaradhya

The smell of acrid acids pulses a pungent odour in the chemistry lab. The lab assistant has already handed us the experiment sheets and the students have begun equipping their lab stands with the required Reagents and materials. I've reserved the bench adjacent to mine for Abhimanyu who walks in late.

"Hey!" I hand him his sheet.

"Are we working on the same experiment?"

"Nope."

"Too bad. I'm very sleepy, to be honest. Don't wanna work up the calculations." He says yawning.

"Animesh has the same as yours, he can help you, maybe," I suggest.

The lab teacher is on leave and the lab assistant decides to let us go early.

"Care to catch a smoke?" Abhimanyu asks

"I don't smoke," I answer embarrassed.

"Oops. My bad!"

"I'll accompany you for the coffee though," I add, trying to fill in the awkward silence.

The place is filled with a balmy air of tobacco and caffeine.

"Hope you don't mind?" Abhimanyu asks, lighting the cigarette between his teeth.

I nod in negation, feeling apologetic at having to inhale the secondhand smoke and suction through the carbon monoxide-loaded death.

The film screening has provided the much-needed distraction from the occasional emptiness that I often used to succumb to. I have also grown extremely fond of Vanshika and Aakash who have sort of adopted me. They've been dating for three years now. Aakash opted for CSE in our college much against his father's desire to opt for an IIT for the sake of a societal tag.

The three of us used to spend our days at the central lawn, the winter mornings resplendent with freshly mowed grass, the sunlight breaking down into tender bokeh through the Kachnar trees, the sharp horizon splitting into neat blues. We used to discuss our favourite movies, characters, and scenes. Aakash felt for the sensitive protagonist in A Death in the Gunj. I would have almost associated him as someone carrying the same personality as Shutu but there are days when I see him indulging in more vocal activities and I admire him for taking a stand by his decisions. The evenings of my time are filled with dinner nights and coffee outings with Abhimanyu.

On the day of the film screening, I woke up drained and sad, unable to pull myself out of the coalesced nightmare that still hung over my thoughts long after I'd bathed. I hurriedly grabbed a loaf of brown bread, spread the fruit jam on it, and rushed out of the mess, finishing the food in two mouthfuls. Vanshika and Aakash are already waiting for me in the auditorium, looking anxious.

"Relax guys." My voice gives in to uncertainty and anxiousness.

After what seems like hours, our movie begins to play. The opening music is spellbinding and I can tell from the expressions of the judges that they seem pretty impressed and curious about our title "The Colour Ochre".

Our theme on gender disparity is going to be acceptable. The story is about a young girl, Aarti, who rebels against child marriage advocates female education, and meets thunderous applause.

The results are announced and to my extreme amazement, we've won the awards for the best screenplay and stunning visuals.

We high-five each other and celebrate the occasion in the nearby lounge.

CHAPTER VII

Musical Atonement

Aaradhya:

Days condensed into January winters. The chilled air cut through the skin even as the midnoon sun dappled across the campus roads, pouring the mild warmth on the Greystones like some milked bleach. The short winter vacations had left us more tired than refreshed. I was irked at not being able to visit home due to the short duration and long journey. I was doing away with the homesickness by reading John Milton for poetic depth and bliss, occasionally chewing through the boredom by reading Elizabeth Wurtzel's dark accounts in The Prozac Nation which left me more seasonally depressed than usual. I spent most of the days trying not to quiver, layering myself under the sheaths of sweaters and hoodies, relieved at the prospect of being able to hide the extra bulges of my body. The winters left me starved and craving, my anxiety piquing at weighing 74 kg. The lectures of the new physics semester were repetitive and monotonous, resplendent with the yawn and drool of collective boredom of a class of hundred engineers. The carcass of the droning notes of the professors, lecturing us like machines who barely suspected or gave a thought to the practical utility of the topics being taught made the routine tense and terrifying. They didn't seem to mind that repeating the high school basics about solar cells and quantum mechanics would not upgrade our pre-existing knowledge.

Abhimanyu was regular with bunking the classes, his attendance running at a threatening low at 27 percent. Scoring single digits in the midterms burdening him with compensation with a higher than average score in the end seems to be able to pass the subjects. The only times that we academically connected were the compulsory labs, writing down experiments in the files, and submitting assignments just a few minutes before the due time.

"Psst" Abhimanyu passes a folder to me during a physics tutorial. I take it into my custody, opening it curiously under the desk. I can almost feel the eyes of the Young physics lecturer on the blackboard, chalking through some uncomplicated derivation, arriving at a rushed complex correlation.

"Why is he teaching this crap again?" Abhimanyu complaints. I look up to see him solving a basic numerical, using the scientific calculator.

"Don't know," I answer, turning the first page in the folder. "Pretty dank and dark, huh!" I gasped, skimming through some very graphic sketches dated in order and signed Abhimanyu in a cursive Devanagari. The charcoal drawings depict scaled sea monsters caught in a moment of motion. One of the pictures is a snake biting off its tail, with fangs cornering the delicate edge of its twisted body in a circle. I smile at the thought of a tortured continuum; the one without a beginning or an end. The next sheet had the picture of raven chickens being fed some gruesome deer meat, spilling out of the beak and talons of their mother. Their eyes shone with greedy anger and hunger. The tender meat was dripping with very life-like red blood, shining in sharp contrast with the multitude of detailed black sketches. I look up confused, raising my eyebrow questioningly at Abhimanyu who grins with an evil edge on his thin lips "Nah, not blood. Would do better next time." He says, placing his hand on my knees, squeezing the flesh gently. I shudder at the feel of his ice-cold fingertips, electrifying through my thick denim. I observe that his nails are a bluish brittle, his fingers slender like that of an artist. He snatches the folder as I try to turn another page.

"The rest of them are a bit disturbing, you'd think of me as a sadist if you see the nudes ahead." He explains lifting a curled hairlock falling into his eyes.

"Yes, Boy?" The professor has stopped teaching and thunders, staring at us. Abhimanyu looks up, shocked.

"Yes you, you the troublesome busy pair." He points and glares at us fiercely.

"Why can't we accept this answer?" He repeats irritated placing his finger on the board, at a double-underlined figure. "What's the issue with this?"

Abhimanyu stands speechless with a blank look spreading like a dumb mockery on his face.

"Get out you fool." Professor retorts "The future of engineering is as bleak as it can get."

Abhimanyu leaves the classroom unabashed and unapologetic, swinging the weightless bag strap across his shoulders, and carrying the folder under his arms. The professor shifts his gaze at me, his ego throttled beyond measure.

"Care to answer girl? Or wanna make it out after him?" He asks with an acidic undertone.

The class turns around looking at me and breaking into hushed murmurs and gleeful whispers. I can feel the blood rushing to my ears, pounding like fire in the blood vessels. I stand up, gripping the edge of the wooden table, looking quickly at the solution on the board.

"Sir, because the percentage error is beyond the permissible limits and stands in violation of Heisenberg's Uncertainty Principle." I guess confidently.

"Yeah, that's right. Watch your company girl." He says dismissing the answer and my existence with a single wave of his hand in annoyance.

I see Abhimanyu's figure retreating towards the adjacent washroom.

The bell rang after what seemed like an entire eternity, I walked to the exit blocked by two boys.

"He wasn't expecting a smart answer." The taller of the two guys speaks, leaning back against the wall casually.

I stare, shifting my focus from one face to another, glaring questioningly.

"Abhijeet Sharma, Chemical Engineering." The taller guy extends his hand and I shake it timidly.

"Rajneesh Singh, Chemical Engineering." The shorter guy with the shy nerdy appearance waves awkwardly.

"Hi. Aaradhya, Chemical."

"Yeah, we know" Abhijeet winks, dimpling his handsome and fair cheeks, flashing a set of perfect pearl teeth.

"Come along, let's eat and get acquainted in the canteen." Abhijeet grabs my arm as I begin to hesitate.

Rajneesh trails behind. Abhimanyu jogs along, slapping Abhijeet's back in a friendly recognition.

"Sup bro?" Abhimanyu punches him gently.

Abhijeet winces, rubbing his ribs where the friendly fist has landed "Headed for the canteen with your girlfriend since you never cared to introduce her yourself."

"I'm not his girlfriend," I interject lowering my eyes, trying to hide the blush.

"Good for you, I guess." Abhijeet cajoles, nodding at Abhimanyu.

The canteen is saturated with aromatic spices and bored students scuttle around mechanically, complaining about inedible mess food and pending assignments. My eyes dart around the place in search of a quiet private spot. The crowd makes me claustrophobic, and I can almost feel my heartbeats palpitate in surrender to a panic. Abhijeet wraps his arm around my waist, pushing me towards a vacant spot for four.

"Go and sit there." He says in a comforting yet flirtatious tone. "I'll be back with my usual order."

I sit on the chair, grab the menu, and run my eyes through the non-appetizing dishes.

"Paneer dosa for me," Rajneesh tells Abhimanyu.

"What about you?" Abhimanyu asks dropping his bag on the chair next to mine.

"Umm...still figuring it out."

"I'll order us some coffee?" Abhimanyu offers at my stretched indecision.

"Yeah, okay!"

"Hazelnut frappe, sounds fine?"

"Dope." I grin in affirmation.

As Abhimanyu walks away to bring our orders, Abhijeet arrives with a plate loaded with pavs reeking with Amul butter and bhaji that smelled suspiciously delicious.

"Ughh....bet this ain't Arabica" Abhimanyu takes a sip from his mug, frothing his moustache, and extends his hand to give me mine.

Abhijeet snatches the mug mid-air, helping himself with a large gulp. "Yum!" He beams with satisfaction, pushing his plate towards me. "Go ahead, take a bite." He offers.

"Very ungentlemanly" Rajneesh says, eyeing Abhijeet in reproach.

I smile, plucking a piece of pav and dipping it in the extra butter.

"Here try this." Abhimanyu hands his mug.

"Tastes bitter and buttery," I say.

We chat for a while, scouring through the crumbs of the leftovers, talking about routine, classes, our whereabouts, and hobbies.

I gather that Abhimanyu and Abhijeet know each other from the same maternal natives and Rajneesh is a dropper who still finds it difficult to readjust and step up his lost self-esteem.

"Abhi I gotta go for real." I stand alarmed, suddenly remembering that I had to go to the office to apply for the scholarship before 5.30 PM.

"Sure" Abhijeet and Abhimanyu shout in unison.

She meant me, I can hear the two guys argue as I leave smiling at the first encounter of the male attention that a female is supposed to receive in abundance in an engineering college.

"Heyaaaa" Abhimanyu says musically one evening, shaking with an excited nervousness.

"What's the buzz?" I ask.

His ice-cold fingers lace around mine and he pulls me closer in a tight embrace.

"Got selected to audition in a city-level event called musical atonement that'll be held in the city square open-air theatre." He whispers excitedly in my ear.

The smell of his Park Avenue marked with a whiff of some other unearthly smell makes me nauseous.

"Congrats," I say freeing myself from his grip.

"Join us, please. We're leaving right away for the practices." He insists emphatically, pressing my hand in persuasion. I follow him towards the central lawn where a group of seven people stand beaming and waving at us. I can only see the familiar face of Abhijeet amongst 2 girls and 5 boys who cross hurriedly towards us, raising his hand in a high five.

"Yeah, congratulations." I applaud shaking my head.

"Nah! Not me. I'm just being a humble supporter. I'm not a participant myself." Abhijeet explains.

"Here's your uke." One of the two girls says handing Abhimanyu a black bag.

"That's Maya, my crush. She sings the chorus and Abhimanyu is the vocalist of course" Abhijeet whispers looking at the girl. "And the sole reason for my cheerleading their band."

"Ohooo" I smile encouragingly.

"But let's concentrate on you for a while." He says sheepishly. "So.....who's your favorite?"

"Ummm.....let me see, I listen to some rock, a bit of jazz, some country, and a bit of death metal too," I say.

"Good God. I was expecting Hindi indies from you ma'am."

"The only Hindi songs that I listen to are the 60s classics from Bollywood. They remind me of my baba." I turn a little grim, breaking off at the memory of a jarred radio pouring sad melodies of ancient love songs and my father humming along as he works.

"Not gonna lie, I suspect you to be the summertime sadness kinda girl." I snap back into the moment at Abhimanyu's voice.

"Huh" I ask, startled.

"She listens to more than you can figure out and impose on her personality," Abhijeet says.

"Would've taken you to be a Lana Del Rey fan, she's the GOAT, modernizing American Nostalgia like people say." Abhimanyu remarks.

"I love her." I agree, embarrassed at being given the sad girl personality already.

Abhijeet and I sit together, watching the band perform. Abhimanyu sits cross-legged on the stage, strumming the ukulele with a coin. His eyes are half open or maybe half shut, I can't make out their crescent transcendence from the distance. His deep voice pierces through the dusk air, in a perfect imitation of James Hetfield of Metallica.

.......I never opened myself this way

Life is ours, we live it our way

All these words, I don't just say

And nothing else matters......

The chorus reverberates through the openness, attracting the attention and admiration of the bystanders.

.....never cared for what they do

Never cared for what they know

But I know.....

My heart melts at the burning passion seeping through their performance. I know what it feels like I think. The place where you can truly belong, without judgment, without imposition.

We often spent the following week, talking about music while the guys smoked.

The Beatles make you sympathetic with their softcore music but Nirvana makes you nihilistic, almost.

We talked about Norwegian black metal bands and graphic movies like The Lords of Chaos. We argued about what parts of the movie about the Mayhem were true and what was fictitious publicity to attract attention from the crime thrill seekers.

I gathered that while Abhimanyu was a die-hard fan of Kurt Cobain, Abhijeet loved Elvis Presley.

We would sing Frank Sinatra

I have got you under my skin

I have got you, deep in the heart of me.....

Orchestrate our little musical fantasies like Ella Fitzgerald and Lou Reed.

We would debate about what death metal bands were the best, howl and shriek till our throats were sore and we fell laughing while practicing metal screams.

Abhimanyu would send me his recorded notes:

Everlong by Foo Fighters, All Apologies - by Nirvana, Fake Plastic Trees- by Radiohead, Passenger- by Deftones.

I'd appreciate the perfect copy of his voice. We shared our favorite songs and our hearts connected with musical symphonies.

One day Abhimanyu called me at 3 in the night, a day after his auditions. He sounded morose.

"I am never gonna participate again." He spoke.

"Hey! It's okay. Tell me what went wrong?" I tried to soothe and distract him.

"They restricted the genre to rap and pop and I had to do an Eminem, the last moment change didn't go as planned."

"Well.....that's not your fault, you can forgive yourself."

"Not feeling too well but I'll have to start working on my independent music soon. Help me write down lyrics?"

"Sure."

CHAPTER VIII

Hello World

The days crammed into a gigantic oneness, merging into one another without a distinct outline separating the night from the day. Sakshi and Ishita almost always stayed out and busy. Dinisha was my only constant source of worry and irritation. For 8 months she had been a migraine with her undisciplined habits. She would barely take turns cleaning her room, eating chicken biryani in bed, and creating an odorous mess. Her high shrill voice would often wake me up in the middle of the night while she fought with her boyfriend unashamedly screaming derogatory terms in her language. I had to bury myself deep in the pillows and I often woke up even without external triggers, sobbing after dreaming about my dead father. Dinisha indulged in excessive tiktok making by the day, wearing mismatched revealing dresses, moving about the room and the halls in a self-absorbed narcissism. I don't understand the dopamine rush that people get through virtual validations. As the count of her followers increased online, the hatred for her disturbing tendencies and cheap publicity rose.

Ishita continued her rhythm of dating and dumping guys monthly, earning her the reputation of a whore, which neither of us considered an insult.

"I don't wanna settle for someone dumb or misogynistic or average looking." She would complain and we would agree in a manifested unison.

Free world, of course. You do as you like.

The stories and stigma grew really serious after she tried to win back a guy (Akshat Singhal) by giving herself very light yet disturbing scratches on the forearm.

Sakshi and I spent the next few days, cooking Maggie and Macaroni for her, wearing wet clothes to bring down her anxiety-induced fever. We got to know that she was allergic to cetirizine and sensitive to dolo-650mg, so we had to make the compensation with her orders for dark chocolates and ice creams. On 14 February, our room was reeking with the fragrance of red roses sent by Akshat Singhal to Ishita Mullick, marking one week of their dating phase.

People walking with their eyes glued to the screen, surfing, swiping, scrolling, and smiling idiosyncratically was a common sight. Even those of us who had barely managed to code "Hello World" in the first year could be seen clicking the keyboards noisily in the computer centers, living in cyberspace isolated from reality.

Yet another class of highly ambitious individuals spent hours arguing and believing in Elon Musk, Stephen Hawking, Bill Gates, Jeff Bezos, and family and moral values all alike. These people would spend the day hours worrying over some silly indentation error in their unending codes and work their asses off by the night, competing to upgrade their profiles on geeks4geeks, code forces, and other head-wrecking anomalous platforms. The only reality for these people was safely wrapped between glyphs and ASCII codes.

Another group was that of the average scorers, who invested (rather wasted) their time and attention equally in trying to find a perfect date, keep up with their long-distance relationships in some other cities, or indulge excessively in sports and extracurricular co-curriculars. This group was also inclusive of the heartbroken, hard-to-impress gym freaks whose sole purpose in life was to attain six-pack abs and rippling muscles and break the heart of every other girl.

The engineering outcasts were the students who kept themselves as high as a kite. Scoring weed and hashish by the day and spending the nights on the topmost terrace of the buildings, getting stoned while stargazing. These damaged people were not so dense in population but were too far gone. I'd known people who couldn't write down the examinations without rolling a joint first, the seniors who couldn't sit for the interviews unless they had ingested a fair amount of cannabis.

It helps with the anxiety bruh! Sharpens my memory. They would answer in the advocation of their addiction.

Ah! Do you see those colors? I can see the music dripping. Can you, can you see that door between those trees, I can one hundred percent bet that it's a portal to the alien world.... The psychedelic dissolution of life was a fair answer, warping them up in a safe untraumatized bubble.

All these groups, clubs, and social circles yet I could never find my fit and belonging. The more I read, the more isolated I felt. All I knew was that everyone was a little bit depressed deep down, masking it with the engineering fatigue and the farce of having aced one of the toughest examinations once. The world around me neatly polarized into: the ones who didn't know themselves and what they were doing and those who knew themselves too well to know that they were trapped in the wrong place.

I mildly suspected Abhimanyu to be a stoner and when I asked, he answered affirmatively, much to my dismay.

"Started after my dad died before JEE Advanced." He spoke grimly. "I didn't wanna spend the nights trying to think about what would happen. Couldn't see my mother and my sisters cry. It was the only way to keep me unemotional yet energized enough to solve calculus and read typical organic chemistry. Curtis's rearrangement and the Interference patterns made sense only when I was high."

I could oddly empathize.

I'd tried to create an Instagram account for a second time now when the seniors of the Literary Club had quite literally forced me to publicize our magazine and content online. Almost all the people that I was friends with would insist time and again that I needed to be on social media to keep up with the trends of memes and reels (none of which made any sense to me either way). I signed in with a made-up username @darck_amen09, sending a friend request to former classmates from school and coaching. Abhimanyu tried to teach me by archiving the posts that I no longer wanted to keep on my profile and I told him that I would never have the guts to post in the first place. He laughed dismissively "One never knows."

Life seemed discreetly distant even online, a fake narrative of a fantasy self. If the world was so full of happy and perfect people, why did I only ever see the mechanic zombies doused in a workaholic callousness of engineering academics?

As desperately as I tried to shuffle and morph into one of these GenZs the more alienated I felt. I wondered if it was because of the Christian schooling that left me so aloof, discontented, and disconnected. The only sex talk and sex education that I could illuminate was by recalling the sentences of my school principal, " Your body is a temple of God and you shouldn't mutilate it with self-pleasure or premarital sex."

Ishita often returned late in the mornings, smelling of cheap hotel shower gels and sickening bedsheet perfumes, chirping excitedly about the best meaningful sex ever. I could never relate to any of her talks but listened to her patiently.

I found out that Abhimanyu was mission schooled too, in a co-education day boarding thankfully. We would often recite the Lord's prayer and assembly hymns and Christian rocks to recall our memories that now receded away into some forgotten distant times.

I would often go to the basketball court in hopes of catching the sight of Abhimanyu playing. But I gave up after a few days because I couldn't master perfection at once (anybody could tell that my expectations of myself were unrealistic). Also, I felt unathletic due to my massive bulk and stubborn fat that dislodged into body dysmorphia.

The mornings were spent in the Lecture halls, the noons in the labs, and the evenings in Abhimanyu's smoking company. The nights were always the most cruel. I dreamt about my father and woke up trembling, crumbling under the weight of a crushing breakdown. One night I dreamt of my four-year-old self in a green meadow listening to my mother reading out from Grimm Brother's fairy tale books. I was acutely aware of my father's presence somewhere in the fields even though I couldn't see him. As my mother finished reading the happy ending, I saw a red velvet Savan ki token perforated on the glazed sheet of the book. It began to dissolve into the words and metamorphosized into a smiling picture of my father. Soon the book was transformed into floating happy childhood images of me and my father. I clutched the book, hugging it to my tiny chest.

When I woke up, it took me several minutes to comprehend that it was only a beautiful dream, thereby dismissing the Freudian memory as too kafkaesque to be real.

Dinsiha was looking at me worried and I realized I'd been crying all along. I sat up in my bed, wiping the corners of my lashes, and gulping hot water from Dinisha's bottle.

That day I concluded that I didn't belong in the present, neither in the real world nor in the virtual one but was a creature of the past where all the fond memories were still real and my father was alive in them.

CHAPTER IX

If the world was ending.....

It's been a few days since Siddhartha has arrived home. Sejal is busy preparing for her upcoming board examinations and rarely leaves her room. Mrs. Sharma dotes on him, taking excessive care to cook his favorite meals: Upama, Poha, Aaloo parantha along with mango shake for breakfast, Bhindi, stuffed brinjal, moong daal and Lassi for lunch, Dosa, idli, pasta, mogra beans and a glass full of milk for dinner. Mr. Sharma has been in extremely high spirits and in a good mood lately. He even allowed Siddhartha to hang out with his school buddies and he ate the famous Kathi rolls and tea from Tarachand ki Thadi, recalling the good old days tinged with a light-hearted humor. His eyes shimmered at the inviting bliss that his hometown offered, extended like a minuscule version of some paradise.

"Sid, let's go for a long drive." Mr. Sharma offers one day, much to everyone's astonishment.

"What? Where to?" Siddhartha asks, taken aback with a mild surprise.

"Wherever my boy wants. Just you and me and the world."

"But Dad, what about college? I only came here for a week."

"Oh you rogue, you better be kidding, huh? Do you attend all those lectures?" Mr. Sharma guffawed. "I was your age once."

"Umm....sure!" Siddhartha grins in agreement.

The father-son duo embark upon the journey in their white Fortuner racing smoothly towards Mussoorie. Mr. Sharma drives cautiously and jovially. They trek, they eat in their favourite restaurants and food stops, they laugh and they talk almost like lost friends. They talk about ordinary things, they talk about new construction sites changing the landscapes, they talk about politics, they talk about cricket, they talk about future and finance, and almost about everything that they can possibly think of. Years of bitter ice seem to be cracking away at the sound of their humor and fervor.

"Sometimes I feel sorry that I didn't give you enough time as a kid." Mr. Sharma laments retrospectively.

"It's alright Dad. You were posted away." Siddhartha soothes him.

The evening sun starts to sink low, spreading vermillion patches over the hilltops. At this altered altitude of the Lal Tiba, every cloud, every seething emotion feels tangible. Like you could reach out your hand and stop the time, stop the feeling, grab it forever. The cedar trees lined infinitely like a green army spaced evenly in the continuum of a thoughtful discipline. The gorge below expands in a generative width, the light breeze makes everything flutter in a lost-and-found desire.

"Most fathers would take pride in teaching their kids basic maths and sciences. But I'm glad that I could teach you discipline and the necessity of engineering." Mr. Sharma places a friendly hand across Siddhartha's shoulders. "I was shattered when you told me about your desire to be an artist." He shakes his head in dismay. "C'mon you had to be practical, you needed to be realistic I thought to myself. How could I let an army officer's son seek the insanity of art? The idea was simply preposterous. All those colors in your room were a blotch to my reputation and ego. Art can't earn you money, my lad. But I'm sure that you understand me better now. I hope you know that I did things for your best."

"Yes Dad, I know better now. It's nothing more than a pastime hobby." Siddhartha spoke, for once feeling the warmth of understanding and respect.

"Oh, that shall pass too. It's just an added accolade for your resume, nothing more and nothing less."

"Let's drive back now, it's getting late," Siddhartha suggests urgently, looking at the last receding streak of sunset.

"Never mind the dark son. The night belongs to us. I will drive ourselves in the morning after we see the sunrise. I still remember you complaining as a little kid, about how I'd never taken you to Mussoorie despite it being within the driving vicinity of Dehradun."

They decide to spend the night in a decent two-storeyed hotel, perched like a bride's brocade on a ledge.

The far-stretching wilderness of the night gave a sense of resolute barrenness.

They ordered Siddhartha's favorite Rajma-Chawal, Kadai Paneer, Tandoori Naan, and Rasmalai. They ate sumptuously and slept like kittens in the hotel bed.

It is a beautiful evening. The sky is a strange shade of bronzed lavender with a few shards of smoky clouds scattered across its colossal belly. The beach is exploding with happy families, jeering and singing happy rhymes. The little kids are running around with Ferris wheels, some are making sand castles and seashell jewellery. Siddhartha has a lavender candy floss made out of a piece of the sky. As he takes a bite, it melts like sugar threads in his mouth, spreading a satisfactory grin across his face. Sejal's gotta try this. He thinks to himself. But where is she? He looks around confused. The beach people start running frantically, screaming, "The world is ending, it's ending in purple tides." He looks around at the panic-stricken people holding the hands of their loved ones, dashing safety. Oh God! Oh God! If it's the last day, I want to die with my family. Siddhartha runs along thinking. A gigantic purple tide leaps and engulfs him before he can catch hold of his parents and sister. He feels suffocated, the saline cotton-candy-like water glues his scream. Hot tears sting down his cheeks and he wakes up drenched in sweat.

The surroundings of the room shift into an unfamiliar outline and it takes him a couple of minutes to gather that he's in a hotel room in Mussoorie, on a trip with his father. He turns his head to find Mr. Sharma's bed is vacant and his phone is still plugged into the charger. Siddhartha stands and douses himself with water, gulping its coldness greedily. Where is he? He thinks as he opens the drawer and finds his father's handkerchief and car keys, ascertaining that he couldn't have ditched his son. The lock screen displays 2:36 AM. Siddhartha checks the washroom and is surprised to find the door ajar. "Dad?" He asks in the empty air. "Dad?" He repeats with a weighing concern.

Siddhartha steps out of the room. The yellow lights pouring into the hotel gallery give the surroundings a foul, pungent, sickening pallor. There are rows of unoccupied rooms except for the one at the farthest corner. A familiar manly voice and cat-like moans erupt through the silence. Siddhartha taps at the door of the room. The noises in the room died down. After what seems like infinite knocks, a woman in her late thirties opens the door, an unlit cigarette dangling from her fingers. Her hair was scanty across the breadth of her almost bare collarbone. "Yes, kid?" She asks, adjusting the loose see-through dress, attempting to hide her protruding breasts.

"Oh! I'm sorry." Siddhartha turns around ashamed. "I was looking for my father."

"Ummm....no one's here." The woman replies, lighting the cigarette.

As Siddhartha begins to walk away, he hears a shuffle in the room, he makes a sharp turn catching a glimpse of his father as the woman hurriedly slams the door shut on his face. He stands traumatized at the sight of his father sprawled stark naked on the bed, mirroring his son's look of horror and disgust.

This can't be true. Siddhartha keeps repeating to himself as he walks back to his room, trying to forget the events of the night. He crashes on the bed, drained of energy and emotions. His arms flailing at his side, devoid of rage and loathe. This can't be true. His head pulses with the recent images, coursing like a migraine. He takes out Disprin tablets from his pocket and takes two at once. He takes down three more as the ache refuses to cease. At the crack of the dawn, his father enters the unbolted room quietly. He asks Siddhartha to get ready for home.

There is no home. It's my last ride home with this man. Siddhartha's head is splitting with ache and disgust. His eyes contoured with swelling, pupils dilated with overmedication. He raises a finger, feeling the throbbing across his temple.

"You look awful." His father barks with eyes fixed on the road ahead.

Siddhartha doesn't say a word.

"It's this passive-aggressive silent treatment that checks my patience. This is exactly how your mother behaves. This is exactly why our marriage is wrecked, pushing me to the throes of alcohol and whores. " Mr. Sharma snorts as an explanation.

Siddhartha's head spins in a violent implosion. Thousands of thoughts and images muddle like a torpedo. He digs his teeth into the flesh of his tongue to keep himself from screaming and crying. He turns his head, staring at the trees blurring behind. Why Dad? How could you do this to Mom? How can you ever justify her heartbreak? Why Dad? Tell me this isn't true. This can't be true. He keeps repeating to himself.

"You'd better not breathe a word of this to your mother. You'll be leaving for college but your complaints might dismantle the peace of our house. Sejal's studies will be affected and I won't rest until I see her qualify for AIIMS two years from now." Mr. Sharma says sternly.

Siddhartha punches his thighs aggressively. "It's too much." He shouts.

Mr. Sharma jerks the car to a sudden stop.

"What is this about?" He looks at his son, his eyes burning with anger.

Mrs. Sharma opens the door at the sound of the bell, greeting and embracing them cheerfully.

"How was the trip?" She asks, her eyes on Siddhartha.

"It was great. We had the best night ever." Mr. Sharma interjects.

"Maa, I need to leave for college immediately. An assignment is due for submission tomorrow and I forgot all about it. I can't begin to lose credits already." Siddhartha spoke without meeting his mother's eyes.

He rushes to the room and begins to pack his bag, violently flinging his clothes and books inside.

"What's the matter, Sid?" Mrs. Sharma asks, eyeing her son with sympathy.

"Gotta go Maa. The assignment.....Deepesh called to remind...." He insists tearfully.

"Did your father say something? Did he beat you again?" She asks turning around his hands to look for the marks of violence.

Siddhartha broke off the hand from her grasp angrily. "What's wrong with you? It's the damned assignment. That's just it."

It's been a week since Siddhartha's unexplained return from his visit back home. His howls and cries have perturbed the routine of his roommates. Upon being asked, he either nods in negation or pushes them away violently. Even Deepesh's sarcastic jokes have ceased having an impact. Vedanta has tried in vain to coax him to smoke. He even tried to offer him a joint, saying, "Might help with the nightmares." but to no avail. Lakshay has shifted into his branch mate's room to code in peace.

Kiran adjusts the glasses on her nose, the feminine perfume wafts like a comforting shelter as she hugs Siddhartha. It's been 6 months and the only solace that he finds is when he is with her. College would've been a nightmare too without you. He often tells her.

They spend the weekends eating in fancy restaurants and listening to music together. As he walks her back to the hostel, they kiss under the lamppost, her tongue stroking his lips with a fragile innocence, spreading the tender warmth shyly. They part with a hug and say I love you to each other as Kiran trembles like a wounded swan, crumbling into his strong embrace.

Siddhartha comforts himself at the thought of having discovered a new home in her feelings through love. It makes him bound and safe. Lately, his life has started to revolve around Kiran. He is obsessed with her thoughts and tries to picture her routine and life. He wants to know her all at once. He wants to atone for his sins by committing to her. Siddhartha knows the lyrics to each of her favorite songs. He makes sketches to impress and win her smile. His pencil traces the sketchbook with a marked perfection, lining the large set of deer-like eyes, shading each and every familiar curve and curl on her face, the angular chin on a round baby face. Every minute detail brings his sketches to a severe life, radiating vivacity in their creator. The fact that she's two years older than him and that the relationship might lack a future doesn't seem to cross his mind at all.

One afternoon as Siddhartha walks out after the Mathematics class, he catches the sight of a familiar white kurti. Kiran. He recognizes her happily. Just as he decides to make a dash and lift her up, he's stopped dead at the sight of another guy talking to her. The guy pulls her closer and they break into a passionate kiss. Kiran rises on her toes, burying her face at the nape of his neck. Siddhartha stares at the disgraceful love, his trust shattering into lament and remorse. The sight foraging like a permanent failure, scaring his heart for life.

Later that evening, a part of Siddhartha is splitting with an insane desire to set the world ablaze and the other part of him is too tired even to cry.

Kiran finally calls him back after his 38 desperate missed calls.

"Hello?" Her familiar voice resplendent with a fake cheer.

He's disgusted at the normalcy in her sound.

"Why Kiran?.... Why?" He asks, stammering, unable to keep himself from crying.

"I can explain. It's just that you're really great at sketching. You're a great company. I don't wanna lose you. Mrigank means nothing to me. He's just a classmate. We're nothing serious. He's been trying to date me since the first year of our college....."

"I trusted you." He breaks her off with a soul-shattering sob. "It's over."

"Sid. Wait. No...."

He cuts the call before she could finish her sentence. He blocks her from everywhere.

In the days and nights that follow, he paints obsessively and excessively on his canvas. The memories and the dreams of purple tides, tighten around his neck like a noose.

CHAPTER X

An alternative repository of love

Aaradhya:

Abhijeet was the life and cynosure of every social event, his personality and charm resplendent with a bright sense of humor and dashing good looks. I was mildly surprised at the pace with which our friendship had acquired trust and comfort. I'd begun to confide all my secrets and anxieties, using him as my human diary. Be it my social phobia or examination induced panic attack, there wasn't a problem that he didn't have a solution to. I walked to him like the photographic negatives and he turned them into pretty Polaroids with his silver bromide-like advice. Even though we didn't spend a lot of time together, owing to his unplanned adventure sprees and impulsive tours while I stayed busy with classes, literary club, routine and reading.

One day I called him in a conundrum, he gathered the tone of seriousness in my voice and tried to lighten up the burden.

"You sound like someone about to confess." He remarked, suppressing laughter.

"Yeah? Confess what?"

"Either love or crime. In your case, both are an equal likelihood."

"Haha, so funny. You humoured me so well, I'm touched." I said irritated.

"OK, now come on I gotta see the look on your face while you say it."

A few hours later we were sitting in the central lawn, watching Abhimanyu practice his guitar and vocals onstage.

"I think I like him." I dumped suddenly.

"Wait. What?" Abhijeet nearly screamed in disbelief.

I looked around embarrassed, trying to mask my furtive glances with a casual one.

"Yeah!" I shrugged. "Shhh"

"And what does he say? Does he like you back too?"

"I haven't told him yet. I'm too scared. Besides just look at him...." I say admiringly like a fangirl ".....I mean, a guy like him isn't supposed to be single. He's been a magnet of crush confessions of seniors as well. I don't stand a chance."

"You shouldn't jump to conclusions. Besides you guys seem to team up really well. Discussing all those reticent topics that do not make sense to half the world." Abhijeet said encouragingly.

"Are you sure?"

"Yeah, I mean I was expecting something better from you, like for a sec I felt self-obsessed enough to think you were gonna ask me out on a date and it's been a shock, but wish you luck." He winks at me.

A few days later, Abhimanyu stopped attending the classes and labs entirely. He's flunked all assignments and file submissions. He has wiped out all his online existence, except for a YouTube video of him performing some Parkour trick across the hostel terrace. The WhatsApp text that I sent him three days ago still shows a single tick. His phone has been switched off too.

I called Abhijeet in a rush of anxiety.

"I think he's going through something." I can't keep my voice from quivering.

"Relax babe, I'll check in on him in the hostel and find out for you."

Abhijeet diverts the seriousness to other lighter gossip, relaxing my racing thoughts.

Later that night Abhimanyu texted me

Sup?

Hey! Where the hell is u????????

Hostel. Room. XD

All cool????????

Yeah! Great!

I type and retype until he sends a question mark.

?

You've deactivated your social media accounts and I can't seem to reach you anywhere.

Yeah. Sorry. I mean to explain.

Please do.

Been preparing for the SATs, final this weekend. Was studying.....mock tests n ol.

The text lands like a blow, knocking the breath out of me. It all made sense suddenly. His continued absence from the lectures, his unexplained leaves, his casual coolness for the Academics, his seriousness towards music and basketball. I feel humiliated, betrayed, and angry all at once. I read his text sobbing,

Let's meet tmrw. Cafe: Kaafka's Palace. 7.30 PM. Coffee on me. XD.

Sure.

I flung the phone away and curled on my bed underneath the blankets in a dramatic frenzy.

We walk to the designated coffee place, at a distance of 2 km from the campus main gate. I am constantly reminded of a longing absence even in his presence. The winters have already started to leave their subliminal tang with an uplifting candor. The world seems brighter, everything shifts in a sharper focus in Abhimanyu's presence. As we talk about things, I can barely keep myself from thinking he's going to go and I'm going to miss all of this dreadfully. What would campus life be like without him anymore?

The Cafe is largely unoccupied, the smell of intense coffee greets us as we push the door open. We take a chair, surfing through the menu which is resplendent with a variety of affordably fancy flavours: mint mocha, tangerine white chocolate, bubblegum vanilla, Irish hazelnut, dark chocolate roast.....

Abhi orders a cinnamon caramel for himself and a cold chocolate brew for me. We wait for our order, and he tells me about the specialty of each kind of coffee beans: Arabica, Robusta, Liberica, Excella.... I listen to him feeling spaced out and distant. Since neither of us feels hungry, we gulp our coffee in silence. The wall behind Abhimanyu portrays a large painting of a human metamorphosizing into a cockroach. The kafkaesque feeling melts into the silent space between us.

"Congrats," I say breaking the awkward silence after a while.

"SAT results first."

"Expected scores?"

"1470ish in the mocks"

"Decent enough. Chillax" I say grinning, in an attempt to cheer him up.

"Wanna target UCB, NYU, and Brown."

"Neat."

"Would prefer NYU more though. My elder sister is studying medicines there."

"And....?"

"Will pick computer sciences as the major and music as a side major."

"Uhffffzzz.....I'm so jealous."

As we walk back, I hand him one of my earbuds playing Love in the Time of socialism by Yellow House.

Maybe I'd be better off in Berlin

Or as an artist's muse in London

Drifting from hand to hand.....

He smiles and nods in satisfaction, the moon spilling its silver sheen across his dark eyes and lovely curls.

"Guess what?" He says taking one of my hands in his. "You are a complete vibe." He presses his fingers into my palm gently.

We spend the next few days walking around the campus, eating out and ordering pizzas between the labs, and discussing art and music, and poetry. We work through his music, fooling around in an attempt to find the perfect lyrical rhyme for the rift.

My love is the sweet poison

Makes you swoon

Oh Lover, Oh Lover Lost

Cursed be this boon

Abhi leaves for Delhi to write down his SAT. He phones me later the same evening, his voice brimming with excitement.

Guess what? 1485 it is.

Wow.

Yeah!

So proud of you bud.

Wish you were here. I'm celebrating with champagne. Just picked a chick in Hauz Khas and we're gonna groove in the club.

Have fun.

I talk to Abhijeet expressing sadness and joy at Abhimanyu's plans.

"Guy is rich and ambitious," Abhijeet says

"Yup"

"Why don't you follow him too?"

"No money."

"Ah! What a loss" He says "Don't worry we will earn and fly too. I'll give you my share too babes."

I spend the days trying to distract myself, walking around through the daily drudgeries like a ghost trapped in a shell.

When Abhi returns, he parties most of the time, staying drunk in his friend's apartment outside the campus premises.

One night he drunk texts me for helping him write down his SOPs.

Here's the draft. Give it a read. I need improvisations. Please. XD.

Sure

I text back.

I spend the next few days correcting and elaborating his content, curating personalized essays brimming with keenness and curiosity for each of the three universities. We spent hours editing and omitting the shoulds and should nots in the write-up. We discuss this with our seniors and common professors. Finally, I sent a mail from his account, asking the Dean, the Director, and the HOD for a letter of recommendation for his entrance.

Holi is around the corner and the freshers are going back to celebrate with their families. Deep has called me thrice already to ensure my unfilled arrival for the festival. It would be our first celebration together since Baba's death. I had been trying to avoid going back, not willing to face the traumatic events again but I knew I had to leave. I think about my Maa instead of condoling myself into grief.

Abhimanyu had to rush back home in an emergency. His younger sister and mother met with a minor accident and had to be admitted. The sudden exit, left us without a formal goodbye, leaving me in a great deal of distress.

I walked to the bus station, with my heart heavy from being held like a repository for all the unsaid feelings.

Lockdown

CHAPTER XI

Un–Holi

Aaradhya:

Jodhpur can get desolate and acrid even if you've known it for long enough. Seams of dry land patchy with desert vegetation and cacti, leave you with an emotional erosion. The unending sandy landscape with rounded dunes, and the sky somber with penetrating blues even during mid-noons almost make the scene look like an inverted ocean. Women in Rajasthani lehengas with faces buried in veils and men walking around with a turban on their head look like sea urchins and anemones, floating fluidly. It's a pacific world trapped in itself. Even the March is hot here, providing a miraged sense of self. The day has already started to fade into a slumbering dusk by the time I hire an auto rickshaw from the bus station. Coming back to my hometown is like rewatching a distant dream. The city carries a loathsome sadness sedimented under its land, a twisting unease layered below its dusty airs, a shady thrill lurking under the shadows of khejri, hingot, babool, peepal, mureli. I have already begun to dislike the distance of the new home that Maa bought 3 months ago on heavy installments. It's going to be my first visit to the new place, situated on the very outskirts; this means I have to travel through the crowded streets. I try to look past the food stalls where my father used to bring me to try the best matka kulfis, dosas, and pav bhajis. I try to look past his ghost-shaped memories hiding in every recognizable spot. I try to look past the fathers carrying their daughters in their arms. I try not to mourn for the things that have been beautifully lost.

Every town is a prison

Every walk is a fight

When the ghosts don't leave your back

For a second time....

My brain inadvertently plays Don't Kill the Streetlights as I sit reminiscing the loss.

Maa is waiting for me at the entrance and she runs like a child towards me, flinging her arms around my neck. I hug her and kiss her forehead. She looks at me, her eyes welling with tears. Her tattered green saree clings tightly to her fragile frame. She looks thinner and older than before. Her features are devoid of any jewelry (not because she's been widowed but because they've always been an unaffordable and unwanted luxury to this humble soul). The small gold bangle and a tiny nose pin that she'd got as a dowry were pawned long ago to meet my coaching expenses.

"I'm so glad to see you. I'm so proud." I'm so proud. I'm so proud. She keeps muttering under her breath. I hugged her again. "It's okay Maa."

Our new home is a cemented box of two very small rooms one of which is being used as a kitchen. The BPL television without a dish is sitting unused in the corner. I remember watching the Ramayana and some stupid science cartoons on the Doordarshan. Maa brings me a bowl of Halwa, garnished with coconut fillings, cardamom, and dry fruits. I look at it with a ravishing hunger, greedily burying myself in the melting aftertaste of desi ghee.

"Where'd you get the ration from Maa?" I was surprised.

"We can afford everything now, don't you worry my child. Just enjoy the dish."

There is a gentle rap at the door and before either of us can answer, a middle-aged woman walks in shouting "BhabhiJi". She looks at me and says again "Guddu?" more as an information rather than a shocked inquiry.

"This is Mrs. Vandana." My mother introduces her. "She's been willing to meet you ever since I told her that you're pursuing engineering. Her son is preparing for JEE'20. We thought you could give him some tips."

I gape at her with my mouth open and the spoon of halwa dangling mid-air in my hands.

"Uhmm....huh" is all I manage to say while pushing away the bowl of unfinished halwa to a side.

"I mean finish eating first my dear. We have all the time in the world. Geet hasn't come back from coaching yet." Mrs. Vandana says, eyeing the bowl.

"Here" my mother fills a new bowl for her. "Try this and tell me if it tastes fine."

"BhabhiJi, no need to be formal." Mrs Vandana very nearly snatches the bowl from her hands while trying to stay courteously refusing.

I try to suppress my laughter.

The two women talk about the changing weather, and home remedies for treating hair falls, dandruff, cough, cold, and fever (I begin to wonder if these two should already be designated as qualified doctors). They fill in each other with local gossip. Once they are done, they turn their heads towards me, eyeing me with a doting motherly affection.

"Geet doesn't study at all. I don't know what to do with him anymore. Your mother here tells me that you used to study for 7 hours apart from coaching. Geet stays awake all night and sleeps all day. We've forced him to join two extra tuitions for physics and maths but his scores keep dwindling after every practice test. If he continues like this, I'm pretty sure he will mess up his board examinations too." Mrs. Vandana complains in a breathless monotone.

"Maybe you can guide him," My mother offers sympathetically.

"Don't worry Aunty, I'll try my best," I say.

I beam inwardly at the recognition and respect that one achieves for clearing tough exams and making it into reputed Technological Institutes.

After Mrs. Vandana leaves us with a promise to drag Geet by his ears on their next visit, Maa and I start preparing dinner. I cut the vegetables and she guided me on the amount of spices, cooking oil and water to be used. Despite my repeated attempts, all my chapatis continue to be hopelessly amoebic in structural rigidity. Maa and I sit down to eat together, she appreciates my cooking even though it's below average in taste. I fill her in with the details of my college life and she tells me about education and home loan. Life seems balanced in its materialistic needs but still lacks the edge on sentimental terms; we try to avoid talking about Baba.

Deep, Anita Bhabhi(his wife), and Palak(their 3-year-old daughter) arrive on Chhoti Holi. The five of us go to the community gathering for Holika Dahan. Maa has forced me to wear a kurta against my pleadings. The festivities begin by singing folk songs around the bonfire. The women circle the high flames, feeding it with barley, maze, corn, and coconut. The oldest community member then pulls out the central wooden frame from the fire, symbolizing unharmed and unburnt Bhakta Prahlada being saved from the incineration due to his goodness and righteousness while Holika(the evil being) is immolated.

My mother stands with her face radiating the reflection of the flames, her hands folded, looking like a haloed saint. I'm touched by her patience and faith in God despite all the hurdles and hardships. I've been rendered into the realms of atheism and a fierce dislike for my religion ever since my father died. But I deeply revere her spiritual beliefs. She's my personal God and my only religion.

On the day of Holi, I wake up to the sounds of pots clanking, Palak wailing, and the anklets of my Bhabhi. The aroma of Gujiya and Malpua rose in an appetizing affluence from the kitchen. Deep is already eating lads as I walk in and greet them. Bhabhi extends a plate of Gujiya and Mathri and I dive into their savory tang. We apply gulaal on each other and celebrate the occasion humbly.

I'm surprised by Vanshika's video call later that morning. Her face is coated with dark colors and she sounds high and happy

"Happy Holi Aaru." She nearly screams.

"What fun, you shouldn't have been missing the college festive." Aakash falls into the frame from behind.

"Happy Holi guys." I reciprocate.

Vanshika gives me a little virtual tour of the ground covered with colors, students raving to the Bollywood songs, boys tearing off each other's clothes and throwing them up on trees. The site looks more like a warzone rather than some festival of colors. The students have managed to smear tar and permanent colors and sneak in Bhaang-filled drinks and edibles despite stringent measures of the authorities.

Well good thing, I'm not experiencing the madness myself. I think.

Siddhartha's phone rings for the fifth time and Vedanta answers the video call from his home.

"Namaste Aunty! Happy Holi" Vedanta says.

"Happy Holi Beta. Where is Siddhartha?"

"Umm....right here Aunty. He is busy with some artwork."

"Oh"

"We would have loved to eat Gujiya made by you. Siddhartha keeps telling us that you're an amazing cook."

"I'll save and send some for you." Mrs. Sharma smiles.

Vedanta hands the phone to Siddhartha while mouthing TALK TO HER sternly.

"Hello Maa," Siddhartha says nonchalantly.

"Happy Holi Beta. I wish you were here. The festival seems so depriving without you. The neighbor's kids have been asking about you." Mrs. Sharma says.

"I didn't get the leave Maa, I'm so sorry. We are celebrating here on the campus itself. The mess committee has made us special food for the occasion."

"But I'm sure you're missing Maa ke Haath ka khaana. And why do I not see any colors on you?" Mrs Sharma asks suspiciously.

"I've bathed again already. And yes I miss you and Sejal too."

"Your dad has gone to Mussoorie too for some urgent meeting and Sejal is studying. It barely feels like a festival." Mrs. Sharma says sadly.

Siddhartha feels a sharp pain in his head, rectilinear with hatred at the mention of his father spending the day in Mussoorie.

"OK Maa, take care. I'll call you again." He cuts the call.

It's almost 11.30 in the morning. Vedanta and Lakshya are standing beside Siddhartha's bed, trying to rouse him up from his sullen sleep.

"You've already lied to your Mom about what a fun time you've had celebrating Holi," Vedanta says. "You might just as well make them a reality now."

"There's no point lying depressed in bed while the world outside is rejoicing," Lakshya adds.

"Don't you dare think that your low mood would suffice as a reason for us to leave you unbothered and uncolored." Vedanta adds irritability.

"Wake up you fool." Lakshya pulls him out of the bed.

Siddhartha has to finally yield to the pleading persuasions and stubborn attitude of his two roommates.

The central lawn is a site of jubilation. Rang barse bheege Gunnar wali is blaring over the speakers in Amitabh Bachchan's iconic voice. A few students are dance acting in the scenes of the song from the movie Kabhi Kabhi. Vedanta is already gulping down Bhaang drinks. Students are throwing gulaal and permanent watercolors at each other. Boys are running around in tattered pants, tearing each other's shirts, screaming and slapping in fervor.

Siddhartha joins a group of dancing freshers, trying to fit into the festive vibe. For once in a long time the adrenaline rush of the energetic movements feels better than his usual bedridden depressive spells. He looks around nervously at a group of Senior girls, dancing adjacent to theirs. It's been a week since he broke up with Kiran. He couldn't keep her blocked anymore. The only progress that he has made so far is in resisting the urge to call or text her. He secretly longs to catch a glimpse of her face while burning with rage to avoid her existence at all costs at the same time.

How could she do this to me? He shivers as he replays the memory of Mrigank and Kiran making out. How could she do this to me? The trauma repeats itself like a thousandfold electric field, torturing his wake. Isn't it unholy to cheat on the people you love?

The faces around him are smeared with colors, blurred beyond recognition. They coalesce into a mass mania of some greater facade of a colored pretense to hide from reality.

CHAPTER XII

The Pandemic Diaspora

Aaradhya:

The people are still hungover with the after effects of Holi celebrations. The global case of COVID-19 ensues threateningly. Before the Indians can react in preparation, the Prime Minister had announced a lockdown for 21 days to curb the surging disease.

The conspiracy theorists vocalising this to be a biological warfare with its epicenter in Wuhan, China. The world powers are attempting to seize power by killing the masses. The Indian spiritual heads are proclaiming it to be an end to the Kalyuga, the rising sins and wreckers pleasures are destined to meet their inevitable calamity. Environmentalists are calling this to be a Natures's wrath aimed at restoring equilibrium.

The students who have stayed back in the campus for so long have started to book reservations for going back to their hometowns.

Deep has agreed to stay back for a few more days on Maa's insistence while Bhabhi and Palak have been sent back to the village. The newspapers are still a burning literary and political enigma over the Citizenship Amendment Act. The supporters are happily brooding over the Hindus gaining control while the opposition cries over the injustice, comparing it to be a fascist propaganda against the Islamic minority. The world seems to be fighting the novel Corona virus while Indians are still bridled over its caste-religion warfare. The Hindu Sadhus and the Muslim Fakirs are already endorsing tantras and jhaadaas for spiritual cleanliness to battle the deadly virus, prescribing Ayurveda potions supplemented with the cow piss as the ultimate medicine.

Mrs. Vandana makes her dramatic reappearance, grief stricken, shaking her head in disappointment. A boy of around 17 follows her reluctantly towards our house.

"This is Geet." She announces even though the introduction is obvious.

"Hi Geet" I say And the boy waves timidly without making an eye contact.

"Don't be shy dear. Aaru is just like your elder sister." Maa says, imposing an unnecessary relationship.

They leave us in the verandah where their erupting voices lamenting the unfairness of the lockdown can be heard clearly. Maa hands us a cup of tea each and some home made pakoras before joining her company of Mrs. Vandana and Deep bhaiya again.

"So....Geet....How's your routine? How are you feeling?" I ask cheerily, trying to make a conversation.

"Ummm.....fine." He says without looking up from his cup.

"Good to know. And coaching? And syllabus?" I try to advance the dialogue.

"Lockdown" He utters the monosyllable as a valid explanation.

We sit in silence, while I rack my brains for ways to make him open up. We watch the flocks of evening birds returning to their nests, filling the skies with piercing chirrups. A black bird with an indigo iridescence and a forked, fish-like tail makes a sharp landing, a few yards from our chairs.

"This one is my personal favorite." He says excitedly, his eyes lighting up.

"Umm.....you mean....the species or this particular bird?"

"Oh! the species, of course. It's called the black drongo. These are best known for their excellent mimicry of the notes and phonetics of other bird species. It is an aggressive protector of its territory."

He shows me some bird photographs that he's clicked on his Android. I appreciate him for his ornithological keenness.

"I want to be a photographer some day." He says dreamily.

"Photography? No, don't you dare get any crazy ideas." Mrs. Vandana thunders from the kitchen, overhearing our conversation. "Your dad is nothing like Farhan Qureshi's Abba in three idiots. We have always looked at you like our financial gain. We won't spend a penny until we are promised a satisfactory return of investment."

"Aaru! Teach him some of the relevant JEE trips and tricks." My mother suggests from within.

I look at Geet and shrug dismissively with a gesture. What can I do?

"What would you like to study?" I offer.

"Umm....organic chemistry, maybe? I can never get it in my head."

I give him an overview of the topics that he should give an extra emphasis to and the right way to study the subject. I teach him the different types of reactions: Sn1, Sn2, elimination, and the ways to distinguish their competing mechanisms. By the time I'm lecturing him on Kolbe Carboxylation and Beckmann Rearrangement, I can identify a look of bored resignation in his eyes.

"Geet just like your black drongo, pardon my metaphor, preparing for a competitive examination is like an imitation game too. When you read a theory, you should grasp the fundamentals and be able to reproduce your learning. Don't resist, try to embrace the depths and you'll understand the subject better."

Deep and I often disagree on politics, he's firm on believing that an engineer's worldview is strictly speaking, zero dimensional. He likes to suggest time and again that I am a complete nerd failing to combat real life.

"Life is beyond books." He argues.

"Oh yes? Then who told you to waste your resources and my energy on my education? I would've been happier grazing sheep in the fields." I retorted much to his amusement.

Maa has started to feel a little light hearted and I see her smile more often these days. She spends time with us rather than teaching due to lockdown restraints.

The only bliss that I find in an alarming death-like plaque is the capacity of this lockdown to bring families in a narrow nurturing space.

Siddhartha sits alone in his hostel room. The premises have been barricaded and not a soul stirs the campus grounds anymore. So far he has successfully managed to get away by saying that he couldn't get the reservation and tickets for Dehradun. He fake promises to go home as soon as he gets one.

"Siddhartha, you REALLY need to come back now." Mrs. Sharma insists emphatically.

"Mom campus is safe. Don't worry."

"Workers migrating to their hometowns have been stopped and beaten. The state borders are being sealed too. Situation is going to get worse, Sid. If countries like the USA, Russia, Japan and China have surrendered and failed to curb the emergency, why do you think India would stand a chance against this virus?"

"Mom, please."

"It's not just about you Sid. It's for our sake now. Wouldn't you want to be with us if some medical crisis arises?" His mother has finally been able to coax him by playing the ace card of emotional blackmail and manipulation.

Siddhartha's father has driven his Fortuner all the way from Uttarakhand to Rajasthan, traversing over six hundred kilometers to bring his son home.

"Your dad doesn't want to risk your life. It's very unsafe even with the masks and all the social distancing. Better to be safe than sorry." Mrs. Sharma said over the phone.

"I don't want to impose my safety as a burden on him, Mom. Why can't you understand?"

"For once, Sid. Just this once. Please, listen to us."

The ride back home is a cumbersome journey. Neither of them has spoken a word over the mandatory formality of how have you been? Mr. Sharma is still fuming over the extra pains he has taken to drive alone all the way. The tempestuous surge in the outer world has punctuated the cavity of their existence, churning like a noxious air, unfit for breathing.

The roads are eerily vacant and the only shifting animations are those of the street dogs, cows and occasional sightings of the shy blue bulls.

Siddhartha looks out of the window, his eyes meeting the deadly pallor spilling over the vista like an foreboding augmentation. The old beggars and poor haggards lie writing in pain and hunger on the roadside. Their sharp eyes bulging out of their wrinkled faces, their bellies shrunken without food. Their skeletal frame, a mark of prolonged starvation. It's a cemetery in the making, an assured mass death. Siddhartha shudders at the plight of these social and economic waywards. His father's car passes unchecked and unfined due to his high government rank and reputation. The state borders have been sealed indeed. The migration workers are bustling at the fringes, flogging in large numbers, begging the authorities to let them cross over.

The Diaspora of the workers moved him to tears. The fucking irony of the world. He thinks.

When they are half way from Dehradun, Mrs. Sharma calls them.

"Please drive slow. Drive safe." She says as a concern. As a caution.

"Oh! Fuck you and fuck safety." Mr. Sharma breaks into his usual fury.

As his parents quarrel over the Bluetooth, Siddhartha cries noiselessly, digging his nails into the palm of his hands to keep down his rage and tears. The argument turns into a diabolical hatred.

"I will kill you the moment I see you." His father threatens his mother.

Siddhartha cowers in terror, wanting to throw himself out of the speeding car.

I want this to end. I want this to end. I want this to end even if it is at the cost of hurling myself out of the car.

CHAPTER XIII

Domestic Bliss

Siddhartha spends the evening on the balcony of his room. The skies pour placidity through their vastness. He's been keeping track of the news, desperate for the announcement of the restoration of normalcy. The bludgeoning effects of his unstable home and the recent effects of an unsettling break-up are a tormenting haunt, too much to bear. He's unable to find peace inside himself. No therapy, psychiatry, counseling, motivation, medication, or religion can make you think a certain way or not think a certain way when you're in the throes of self-destruction.

On the days when he wants to humor himself, he decides to switch his position from self-blame and self-pity to that of indulging in an intense hatred directed at the outer world.

He hates it when his father goes about the routine, existing normally, pretending that the night in the Mussoorie hotel was some figment of a nightmare. He hates it when his mother says I love you to his father, unaware of his disloyalty. He hates it when he has to hide his feelings chew his anger and ruminate in a suffocating silence. He hates it when his mother pretends that they are a normal family bound by love and abundance, refusing to believe otherwise. He hates it when his mother doesn't take a stand against injustice and dislikes it when her children voice out against it. He hates his father's authoritative control disguised as betterment in the name of love.

But even in these sepulchered moments of absolute hate and patriarchal tyranny, a small piece of his personal sky lofting through the balcony soothes him. It's his alternative home, a blissful paradise, where he doesn't have to exist the same way. He's not burning with hatred here. He is not sinning, he is atoning here. He isn't grieving, he isn't burning here.

The dusk envelopes stark colors around two pine trees a few yards ahead, in his line of sight. The hues splatter around in an ethereal variance, a reminder of the world beyond this. The shifting silhouettes with the rustling leaves, and a dark outline contrasted against a colorful backdrop, conveying a sense of strong build, making him surrender to an inner artistic decadence.

Siddhartha sits with his palette and pastels, creating the perfect mix, exacting the colors in the skies. It's been 3 years since he's been doing this, it makes him think that maybe, maybe if he can somehow manage to produce a copy of the Shades in the Sky, he would be able to capture the moment of peace, trap it in time somewhere and it would last forever. He likes the idea of placing a bet and making a bargain for equating colors with emotions. He imagines himself to be a collector of these hues: a magenta against the black pine trees with a low hanging crescent moon between them, a deep honeyed shade just before the dawn break, a bursting sepia before thunderstorm with shaking leaves, a shy pink blotted around the blues, a burning tangerine during early winter mornings, a dominant azure with patches of indigo, a lamp black with leaves shining like slivers of silver under the full moon, a quivering grey when it rains, a fierce red just when the sun sinks a little too far, a poignant sapphire with white clouds and lush emerald leaves.

Sejal lives in a routine of repetitions, seldom leaving her room and the only times when she does so is during dinners. The breakfast and lunch are sent to her study desk as she is strictly told to not raise her eyes from the books even for a moment.

"Mom, you're repeating the mistake," Siddhartha warns Mrs. Sharma. "A good result and high scores don't depend upon the hours invested, productivity is based on interest and energy." He continues.

"She's got a vast syllabus to cover. Unlike JEE, medical entrances need better cramming of the theoretical subjects." Mrs. Sharma says defending her decisions.

"But she needs to go out, keep her social life intact. She needs physical activity." Siddhartha continues to argue.

"It's okay bhaiya. It's either a top score or nothing else....." Sejal cuts him off.

It's early in the morning, Mr Sharma has just finished his breakfast and is turning through the newspaper with evident anger.

"Upama was too salty." He snorts in disgust.

Siddhartha walks into the room, still groggy but he can sense the violent energy in the room lurking in the form of his father's foul temperament. He raises an eyebrow questioningly at his mother who mouths all good in a fake composure. He is reminded of the times in his childhood when he used to keep a radar check of his father's moods and footsteps, hiding his colors and sketchbook and himself under the bed on hearing him scream.

He shrugs and goes to bathe not anticipating the gravity of the upcoming turmoil. Thirty minutes later when he steps out of the shower, a towel draped around his waist, his hair dripping with water, he stands stupefied in shock at the sight that meets his eyes. Mr. Sharma is standing over the crouched figure of his mother who is shivering please, I'm sorry. I'm sorry. I'll take better care to not put too much salt. I'm sorry. She whimpers. Siddhartha flung his father away with a violent push, raising his hand in an attempt to hit him back but stopped mid-air when Mr. Sharma surrendered and raised his hands above his head in self-defense from the oncoming blow.

Mrs. Sharma has stood up shakily. "Don't. Siddhartha. He's your father." She begs crying.

Siddhartha refuses to oblige, shaking like a wild animal, torn between the urge to kill and get killed.

"Don't you dare wreck my love, my marriage, and the peace of this house? Don't you dare Siddhartha?" She wails loudly.

Siddhartha turns to face his mother in disbelief. Her hands and neck are severely bruised, and blood flows down in streams from her scalp. Siddhartha walks towards her to examine the wounds. "It's nothing." She says, trying to wipe the blood quickly. "Go back to your room. Now." She commands.

Siddhartha thumps against the wall in his room, hitting his head in anger. As a muddled scream rises through his chest, he turns around and punches the wall in fury till his knuckles bleed.

Why Mom? Why Dad? He keeps repeating with each hit.

Later that evening, Siddhartha is sitting limpid on the balcony, with Sejal beside him.

"When I was 10 years old, I read the news: Man murders his wife, chopping her head brutally with an axe in an impulsive act of rage and violence. He kills himself too. Their two children returned home as orphans.

I used to think that's what our life would be like. One day we would come back from school, step out of the van, and see a hoard of neighbors shaking their heads in condolence. One of them would tell us that he killed her with a knife or set her ablaze and shot himself in the head. We would be the victims living at the mercy of someone else. I used to think that one day I would come back, and there would be no home to walk into. No mother to hug, no father to hold. I died every day, thinking of the death it would cause.

Every night when he would be done beating her and beating us, I wouldn't be able to sleep. I would keep awake, scared, and crying. All three of us cried, trying to hide in the pain, trying to hide the pain from ourselves and one another. While he would snore away in deep sleep, the outburst was just a cathartic act, a way of venting out his pent-up aggression.

I would not be able to tell any of my classmates or teachers about it. I couldn't focus on what they taught in the classes. I would sit mummified and anxious, thinking please God, please God, I want to wake up fine. I want to have a normal life. I want to have a normal father. I want to be a normal girl.

His superiority complex and fake perfectionism, his adamant attitude about being right always, acidified each one of us. It didn't occur to him that we lived in his terror, with our happiness corroded. I feel sorry that all these years, we could do nothing to change him. I feel sad that no amount of tears and words and begging could make him understand.

I never understood why she would protect him and justify his acts. I never understood why she hated us for standing up instead of saving us from his wrath. I never understood the things she did in the name of love. I never understood the things he did to distort that love.

But I felt safe around you Bhaiya. I knew you would protect us. But then you left us too. You stopped calling. You stopped talking. You stopped coming back."

Sejal said without any emotions, looking ahead at the pine trees vacantly.

A few days later Siddhartha opened the door of their house to two figures: his father and the woman from the Musoorie hotel, their faces beaming at him.

"This is Mrs. Anita Divakar." His father says as an introduction. "She is an army veteran, now a practicing doctor. I was very good friends with her husband, the Late Mr. Aditya Divakar." He continues saying, looking at her. She adjusts her pink dupatta and black hair and tries to smile at them with a friendly bow.

"It's nice to meet you." She says in a honeyed tongue.

Mrs. Sharma makes a special dinner for the occasion, extending her polite hospitality to the guests.

"Mom knows." Sejal whispers.

When Siddhartha continues to look at her, confused. She repeats. "Mom knows about her. All about them."

"No, it can't be true. She doesn't know." Siddhartha says.

Mrs. Sharma leaves to bring dessert from the refrigerator and Siddhartha follows her.

"Here let me help you." He says, garnishing the cold kheer with dry fruits and Kesar.

"Mom....umm....I need to tell you something." He says hesitantly.

"Yes, beta?" She asks smiling.

"Umm....I'm sorry but Mrs. Divakar and Dad...."

"I know." She cuts him off curtly, picking up the tray laden with bowls, and walks out of the kitchen.

Siddhartha stares after her in disbelief.

CHAPTER XIV

I float above, above this earth so high

It's a scorching noon, Sejal is sitting on a bench, wiping her sweaty hands on her skirt, shaking her right leg nervously. The school premises are deserted. She searches through her bag: A textbook of physics NCERT, a DLP module for chemistry and two spiral notebooks, a couple of pens. She thrusts her hand deeper and fishes out a folded paper. She takes two sips of cold water from her bottle to keep herself from shaking. It's the same bench, her favorite spot throughout her school days, where she used to read books during recess. It's also the same bench where she used to sit with her brother while waiting for the school van. It's the same bench where she used to sit and watch the seniors train for swimming sports until she became one of them too. It's her favorite spot that she hasn't sat on for quite some time now. It's the same bench where she is sitting for the last time today.

She has waited for so long, so patiently. But in the last few days, her desperation has piqued and her hopes have run out. The COVID cases have risen exponentially, people are dying everywhere, dying unnamed, unidentified, untreated in the homes, in the hospitals, and on the streets. A simple cough, a runny nose, and a mild fever turn into a pulmonary disease overnight, creating oxygen deficiency, and increasing the body temperatures. More than the physical fatigue, the disease has incinerated the mental health of those affected.

The country is turning into a graveyard. The examinations have been postponed until further notice. The wait wears her off. All that she's ever wanted is to be normal and have a normal life. The simplicity of the desire seems unattainable to her now. Her phone rings and she checks the mail: Dear student, congratulations,......She skips through the rest of the content and sees her marks; Physics: 97, Chemistry: 92, Mathematics: 99. She forwards the results of the pre-board examinations to her parents, unable to feel any joy or hope at the prospect.

She unfolds the piece of paper in her hand running her fingers over JUNIOR NATIONAL AQUATIC CHAMPIONSHIP, 2020. She looks at the pool with longing, the blue vastness of the skies perforating a reflective vision in its depths. She stands looking at the tiles below, rising through a shallow refractive haze. A wave of summer breeze creates ripples on the still waters.

You need to quit swimming now and focus on your studies. These two years are the most crucial time of your life, her father had said.

She obliged by giving a false medical report to her coach as an excuse for the inability to continue. She was afraid to tell anyone that she was being forced to quit. She was sure nobody must've been forcing her but she needed to fix her life before she could dream anew. She couldn't think of things that didn't line up with what her parents wanted.

She stood quivering by the pool, inhaling the chlorine-saturated air. She looks at the 10ft depths with an apprehensive longing, a plunging desire.

The past few years flash a fast-forwarded video through her head. Her mother was beaten and humiliated, and the look of disappointment on her father's face if she failed to get what he wanted her to.

Sejal you have to clear NEET with a good rank.....If you continue like this, you'll end up failing me too just like your brother.....I wish I'd just wed you off instead of spending on your education...... Why aren't you first on this test?....... Do you have a boyfriend? Are you planning to run away?

She shuts her eyes and covers her ears to shut out the voices and the images, but they don't fade. The snapshots of the hurt keep ricocheting like some misguided movie with a mixed timeline. Tears trickle down her eyes into the pool. She takes a deep breath, mutters I am sorry and takes a lunge forward. The water splashes out, reverberating a crashing echo through the halls of the isolated building.

"It's not typical of her to stay out this late." Mrs. Sharma eyes the clock apprehensively, checking her phone for a hundredth time for some kind of call or information.

"She'll come back," Siddhartha says as an assurance more to himself than her. "Perhaps she's stuck somewhere."

"It's 9.30, she's never stayed out this late. She could've at least called. She hasn't answered any of the missed calls or texts either." Mrs. Sharma says, pacing about the room anxiously.

"Where'd she say she was going?" Mr. Sharma asks again.

"She said she was going to the coaching to collect the modules of some fresh study material and she said that she'd stay back for a doubt session being conducted for the students who can make it offline." Mrs. Sharma informs again.

"Coaching in the lockdown? You must be insane." Mr. Sharma says.

He calls the administrator of the coaching academy.

"The syllabus was finished 3 months back. They don't have any further notes to add. There have been no doubt classes scheduled for today in any of the batches. And Sejal has not been to the academy." Mr. Sharma tells them.

"This can't be true." Mrs. Sharma says.

"Oh! This has to be true. She has probably run away with some boy, all because of your stupidity and carelessness." He shouts.

Mr. Sharma calls Sejal's coaching mates and school friends.

No uncle, she's not with me.

Haven't seen her in so long.

Haven't talked since the lockdown.

The last time that we talked was three days ago on the text.

No, she hasn't come to my home.

All of them answer negatively, nobody knows about her.

"At what time did she leave?" Mr. Sharma asks.

"At around 11.30. She even sent a mail of her marks scored in the pre-boards. Oh God, I was so proud of her." Mrs. Sharma breaks down saying.

At pre-dawn, the landline telephone sends a sharp shrill in the living room of the Sharma family. The three members have stayed up, tired and resigned. The silence of the night had only been punctuated by a wailing and howling dog, sending blood-curdling noises. Mr. Sharma strides towards the phone answering "Hello?" The voice at the other end says something and Mr. Sharma's face turns ice pale. Mrs. Sharma looks at her husband terror-stricken.

"Who was it? Where is Sejal?" Siddhartha asks expectantly.

"She's been found....pool.....school premises....." He stutters, unable to complete the sentences in any comprehensive way.

Two police constables, Mr. Sharma and Siddhartha are standing at the poolside staring at Sejal's slender body lying morbid in the pool. Her soft brown hair sputtered around her head in little curly waves, her eyes grazing the skies above, her lips tight shut, her face devoid of any sort of human emotion. Her marble-like hands flailing at the sides are open and turned upwards. A few oak leaves lay scattered around her body. The pool is murky due to long absences in maintenance. Her white shirt and long skirt have trapped air across her stiff body. The morning sunrays set the waters in a vermillion dissolution. The light splits her face in a gradient of golden-orangish hues, making her look like a still from some Art Gallery as John Everett's Ophelia drowned in grief and madness.

Siddhartha sits on the living room sofa with the television turned on mute. Mr. Sharma has gone to the police station. Mrs. Sharma has been hospitalized. She lies in a comatose in the city hospital, fettered with oxygen vaults and glucose drips, wailing in fits upon regaining consciousness in intervals. Siddhartha has been asked to answer the calls and attend to any relative or neighbor as and when they care to arrive.

I died thinking about the death it would cause. But you left us. You stopped talking. The words of their last conversations play through his head like a voice note left on shuffle and repeat. He sees flashes of purple tides engulfing and drowning Sejal when he blinks into a short sleep.

It's a terrible accident. One of the constables had said.

But how could it have been an accident? How did they not know that she was an excellent swimmer, a state gold medalist, and a star in the making?

Siddhartha walks into her room, unable to quieten his thoughts. He looks under the raven's picture and finds a photocopy of an unfilled application form: JUNIOR NATIONAL AQUATIC CHAMPIONSHIP, 2020.

Is this why you did it? He asks himself. A young swimmer from Uttarakhand makes the nation proud. An imaginary accolade of an imaginary appreciation makes him smile. You should've waited to see it happen. He cries. You couldn't have been this weak. He refuses to acknowledge her demise. He turns over the contents of her study table, looks through the drawers, the almirah, under the pillow, under the bedsheets, and turns every single page of her books and notebooks a million times, searching for some answer.

She was an excellent swimmer, she was unparalleled, knew the backstroke, and breaststroke, and could pull out butterflies, dive in, and stay underwater with ease. It's not some accidental catastrophe. It's not some thoughtless tragedy, a turn of fate. She did it to herself. She killed herself. She must've been too far gone to have endured the pains of drowning. She must've been broken beyond repair to act on such an atrocious thought, she must've purported her plight in some sort of a pleading. Siddhartha screams. Hitting his head and hands on the walls. Sejal please come back. I'm sorry, I failed you.

In the hollow days that follow, he lives with a void tearing him inside out. He blames himself every waking hour, every sleeping moment: only if I'd talked to her enough, maybe she did it because she was guilt-ridden about Dad's affair just like me, maybe she was too pressurized, maybe she wanted to qualify for the Olympics, maybe she just wanted the pain to end and couldn't see some other way out.

What did the last seven minutes of the brain memory play for her? What fragments was she attested to? Was she peaceful? Did she think about the two orphans who could never go back home? Did she think about the raven in her dreams? Did she want me to come save her one last time?

"She would keep looking for auspicious days to die on, in order to reach the heavens. Little did I know that she meant it literally." Mrs. Sharma says, crying.

"It's not your fault Mom," Siddhartha says in a hollow voice.

Her funeral doesn't have a large social gathering, the flames eat her body in the shadows under a peepul tree in the shamshaan.

They didn't find any last letter or a suicide note. Her phone couldn't certify her reasons for doing it. Mr. Sharma decided to pay off the police and the media to keep the tragedy out of the news and public spectacle. The journalists agreed to write; the army officer's daughter died due to COVID...

"The relatives might think she had an affair and had disgraced herself or that we tortured her or that she was raped. It's better nobody knows about the suicide. It's better if they think it was because of COVID.

Girls like her bring dishonor to the family even in their death." Mr. Sharma said.

CHAPTER XV

The saga of an online world

Aaradhya:

My day began by logging in to the Google Classroom and joining the g-meet link for the online classes. (The lectures were muted until the teacher took attendance). It took a long time to adjust to this shift from an offline to a virtual reality.

No matter how assiduous the professors tried to be while delivering the subjects, the students often shirked their work, were inattentive, and multitasked instead of taking down notes religiously.

The attention span and the patience to understand engineering complexities decreased drastically. The lockdown that began as a method to combat the deadly virus soon turned into an escapist strategy for staying in a personal domain, free from the burdens of work. The world around us came to a standstill while we incubated into a devastatingly lethargic mode.

Every process proceeds in such a direction to keep the total entropy associated with it as a net positive, the limiting value of zero is only reached in the case of reversible processes. The thermodynamics laws that we'd already studied in high school, the universality of randomness, soon propounded a chaotic theory wreaking constant havoc. The basics of the subjects soon changed into un-understandable iterations with rigorous calculations. The Carnot equations, the partial derivatives of the energy balance, had to be modeled into workable codes much to our dismay. The complexities needed us to be more vigilant and vigorous but it became easier for us to shut off the noises with a simple single click on our screens. If we didn't like something, we could cut it off, smile, and not care, accept the virus, which was still beyond our comprehensible control.

We struggled with the online tests despite our resolute faith in the age of digital information, excellent AI bots, search engines with data explosions, calculators, and codes that could solve any numerical. The teachers and examiners had thought of the ease well in advance and they set the papers in accordance. All the shortcut tricks were supposed to fail. Our institute devised its platform for taking the examinations. You couldn't open a new tab on your server, the screens were recorded, the cameras and mics had to be turned on, and the timer wouldn't allow for any extra minutes.

.......The infinite heat reservoir is an abstraction, often approximated in engineering applications by large bodies of fluids. Apply the closed system heat and entropy balance for derivation energy and temperature profiles.

We would wrack our brains searching for the answers online, wasting precious test hours. These could be solved only if you'd studied the basic theory and were comfortable in deriving new results from the fundamental equations. They needed a thoughtful formulation, an intellectual expansion. Teachers took quizzes and viva online with our cameras turned on, asking for reasons behind our answers, and giving us a straight F if we failed to satisfy and justify. Though I found the academic decisions stringent and ethical, I was often troubled when I saw the professors and administration failing to sympathize with tragedies and troubles. If a student lost a loved one, there was no concession granted to skip online tests and assignment submissions. Maybe too much intellectual depth and studies made a person cynical, and the proof lay before our eyes. The world doesn't stop even when you do. Continuum through the change stayed a constant.

Whatever used to be a deductive science in high school, based on simple laws and postulates now became a colossal problem involving complex correlations and conversions. The course expanded to simulations involving new software, I'd started to see my expectations crumbling down into some unexpected reality. This was nothing like what I'd pictured, this was nothing like my fantasy of idealist perfection. I'd started to lose interest in the very subjects that I'd thought would be fascinating. It was a major of my choice and I was struggling, crying while making flow sheets with precise specifications. I ended up being frustrated when the process parameters and components were entered correctly but the results and output were not in alliance with the theory and practicality. The lab work couldn't be performed online and the understanding of distillation columns, heat exchangers, and reactors needed a lot of visualization. All this left me deeply dissatisfied. By the end of the second online semester, I'd seriously started to doubt all my life decisions.

The rising number of COVID-related deaths was an alarming incubus. The people we knew, the friends we liked, the relatives we loved were dying without our last goodbyes, without a proper funeral gathering, without a ritual. We could no longer honor the dead just as we could no longer save all the living.

The tragedies became for real, a nightmarish ordeal while the graduation and academic reality became more and more contrived, a lucid affectation.

The Pandemic that had initially brought the families closer, providing comfort and more time for peace and bondage had now begun to settle into a repetitive routine of habits that looked more like a violation of space, an intrusion of privacy. Members gave each other irritable moods and distress became frustratingly large. As researchers, doctors, scientists, and health experts across the world were looking for a solution in the form of a vaccine, medication, or a miracle, the ordinary masses lived in constant terror.

Dinisha and Ishita would often tell me about how their relationship with their respective boyfriends was being negatively affected. If any love/relationship/friendship was able to survive the lockdown would undoubtedly last longer, they would say. The feelings could not be translated online over the computer and mobile screens. The emotional closeness seemed distant while the insecurities and petty arguments seemed more affecting. As the vulnerability amongst the couples increased, so did the capacity to cut people off at a moment's notice with a single click or a single swipe.

When we video-called our friends and classmates as the only firm connection with the outside world, we would often wonder if the situation would get better someday.

We felt like Anne Frank and Jews trapped in the bunkers and concentration camps with the only difference being that we were forced into hiding and isolation due to a deadly virus and not some fascist dictator. The torture that we endured was not direct brutality and electrocution but in the form of death and despair, our inability to control and fix or reverse the mishappenings.

My college campus life has started to seem like some distant reality, like a dream from long ago, something that I'd only imagined, something that had never been real or would never be real. The only connection that I could sustain from this distant past was in between a few texts and calls that lacked an emotional connection.

Our engineering life wasn't prepared for this online shift, we were being thrust into one, much against our will.

Aakash and Vanshika had managed to rent an apartment near the college and had successfully lied to their families by saying that they were allowed to stay in the hostel and it was much easier to study by staying with others than it would be if they came back home. Their unsuspecting families had readily accepted the fabricated story.

Maa kept the earning and livelihood going by teaching a few students from the neighborhood in our kitchen. So far there have been no reports about COVID and related deaths in our locality. I assisted her sometimes. Mrs. Vandana sent her special Dal-Bati and Churma for us while I helped Geet with his JEE preparation.

Abhimanyu texted me occasionally. He had his hopes high after being accepted into NYU. All his documents had been submitted and he was waiting for his VISA.

"I thought I'd never be able to justify my gap year. All thanks to your help with the SOP." He said over the phone.

"Nah, you deserved it bud," I said blushing with happiness.

We talked for hours, discussing the monotony and distress. He'd told me how he had spent an entire night worrying about his sister's sickness after her accident which had turned out to be a minor viral fever, thankfully.

We talked about the books that we were reading and the TV series we were bingeing. Netflix had quickly become a new normal, an addicting abode to delude ourselves while the world outside shattered with a deafening roar.

"I just abandoned Kafka's The Castle. Too replete and too vacantly abstract. I mean I get the whole idea about feeling trapped but too unrelatable at the time." I said complaining.

"I just finished the trial. It was a tough read and a little less agreeable but ok...." He said.

One day, Deep called us to say that my Nani (maternal grandmother) had gotten sick and her health was worsening every day. Maa worried herself and called a million doctors and Vedas to see if something could be done. It's because of reduced immunity due to old age. They'd say and prescribe medicines that didn't seem to have any effect.

"I'm pretty sure it's the Coronavirus," Maa said, crying.

"Let's go to the village and see if we can help?" I suggested.

Maa and Deep bhaiya made immediate arrangements for our departure. Maa's students had to be waived off from her tuition classes much to the disappointment of the parents. Geet complained that his mental health and studies would be a disaster without my help and motivation. I promised to stay in touch online before we left.

CHAPTER XVI

Blood Bound

Our train sped past the dry lands, rendered even more desolate than the last time I'd been here. As we entered the outskirts of the village, we could see farmers geared up, plugging their lands and I was dimly reminded of Baba again.

We used to spend our summer break in the village when I was a child (before our land met an unjustifiable confiscation). Baba used to carry me on his shoulders around the fields telling me about the various crops and the perfect climate and soil conditions for the best yield.

Moth (dew bean); the pasture legume, sown in late June and mid-July is practically a drought-resistant crop, and can sustain temperatures as high as 45 degrees centigrade. It can be grown on sandy dunes with a poor fertility rate and less organic matter with less maintenance.

Maa would force-feed me cooked moth with curd and chapati almost every afternoon for our stay, saying that the extra protein would be excellent for my mental and physical strength. I would pass the extra sabzi to Baba when Maa wasn't noticing and the two of us would break into a secretive giggle.

Groundnut was sowed as the kharif oilseed crop on our land using our own homegrown seeds. Baba would work meticulously in the fields, perfecting each and every amount of effort in synchronization with the crop requirement. He would take extra care while filtering and sowing the bold kernels.

If the temperatures are low at the time of sowing, the germination will be delayed and the chances of them being infected by seedling diseases can increase. He would say, his back arched over the saplings.

We would store away some of the groundnuts for our consumption and eat them with jaggery during winters, basking in the sunny afternoons.

Baba would nurture the lands with his sweat and blood, freckled and bronzed under the Sun.

The villagers called him the miracle man, the magician who could sprout gold out of the farms. Even during the harshest seasons and pest-infested years, our farm stood out resplendent with high yields. Baba called the abundance the gift of his motherland.

As we passed our paternal landholdings, I was overcome with heart-wrenching grief, at the sight of our barren land that looked even more disastrous in his absence. The last time that we were forced to be here was at the time of Baba's funeral. I was so disturbed and fazed out that I'd blocked all the memories of the grief in a less haunting subconscious vial in my brain. I avoided visiting those dark areas at all costs.

We straight away went to Mama's (maternal uncle) house when Deep came to pick us up from the station.

The house had recently been reconstructed and renovated, with an extension to an additional second floor and a new borewell. The house stood out like some elemental compound in the desert's petri dish. The dunes of the fields rose in a circular bowl around the land, the sunrays slanted along the arcs giving a distant rising obliqueness to the sight.

My Nani lay wrapped in a shawl on a cot in the verandah. Maa was overwhelmed with tears on seeing her. As I bowed to touch her feet, Nani smiled in an effort to recognize and bless me. Maasi (Deep's mother) wrapped me in a long and loving hug. Her yellow Rajasthani dress smelled like Musk melons and baked wheat. I inhaled deeply, surrendering to the best-prized memory from my childhood that I had associated with this fragrance. I knew I was Maasi's most loved and spoiled girl, and she loved me more than her own children.

While Maa and Nani talked, Maasi took me by hand to see my mother's childhood room. It was my first time visiting these corners of the house that usually stayed locked. The small room with multiple racks and slabs in the wall was stacked, rather over flooding with books and photographs. The vintage pictures of Maa, Maasi, and Mama smiling under a Khejri tree, Maa perched on the camel's back with Nanaji smiling in the foreground, Maa receiving a gold medal at her graduation ceremony, Maasi and Mama playing in the fields with the sheep, Maa and Baba's newly wedded photograph. The space overflowed with sentiments captured in frames of her early days. My mother was the first and the only girl to have completed her graduation (in BA-English Literature) from the village, much against the constant opposition and threats from the villagers. But Mama and Maasi had stayed firm on their decision to let her complete the education before getting married.

An archaic smell of old books emanated from the room: Raman Selden's Theory of Criticism, Aristotle's Art of Rhetoric, Barry's Introduction to Literary and Cultural Theory, and innumerable books on Victorian Drama, and Modern Poetry.

Her room was like a museum space as a full stop storing the vacancies from her early life, the books exuding their marked scent in a house that otherwise reeked of milk, cow dung, jujube, snap melons, and cattle. It was the only richness in an otherwise humble hoarding.

I looked around, sniffing in the holy fragrance with a deep tang of longing and jealousy at my mother having lived my dream life. I picked up Maa's copy of Milton's Paradise Lost, reading through her underlined sentences and notes scribbled at the fringes.

"Literature is a madhouse," my mother said on seeing me go through her books.

"I think my interests are rather genetic," I said smiling. "I wish you'd let me pursue this."

"One of my favorite professors had killed herself in a deeply melancholic fashion. You remind me of her. Engineering was your most appreciable decision, considering that we are not wealthy." She said.

"Times have changed ever since your mother. Villagers are now actually proud of you." Deep said, showing me a folded newspaper cutting that he'd saved two years back, containing my photograph and result.

"I would show this to Palak when she grows up. I want her to be inspired by you. I want her to be like you." Deep said.

I beamed with pride, smiling at Mother, after all these years, we were breaking the generational curses and patriarchal mindset.

Later in the night after we'd finished dining; a sumptuous meal of desert beans, kachar ki chutney, ghee-dripping chapatis, and a large tumbler of cow's milk; we dragged our cots in the field under the skies. We talked about village politics, land fragmentation, and related disputes. Nani's health had considerably improved in the last few hours after our arrival, probably due to a healing aura of the family members knitted close.

When I slept under the open skies I saw a million stars clustered together, shining piercingly vibrant, far away from the city's light and dust pollution. I lay tracing and identifying constellations with my naked eyes, soon slumbering into a light-headed and peaceful dream about Baba being alive somewhere in a distant star world.

A few days later, Vanshika called me, sounding dull unlike herself. We chatted about the upcoming endsems and she needed some help with a pending assignment. I assured them that I'd send her mine as soon as I was done. I could sense that she was deeply perturbed and upon asking, she said, "I want to get something off my chest"

"Go on?" I encouraged.

"Umm.....I don't know how to." She hesitated

"Did you guys break up?" I asked, guessing.

"Worse."

"You can tell me, Vanshika, it's okay."

After a long hour of comforting persuasion, she complied:

"I missed three periods in a row, I thought it was because of my PCOD and nothing that should worry me. The last time that we were making love, I told Aakash that it was okay. I was overcome by the heat of the moment and in a lunge of passion I readily lost control. Aakash didn't want to risk it but I forced him to. I am so sorry, I was being so stupid...." She broke into sobs and I waited patiently for her to continue.

"The last few weeks, I used to wake up with a morning sickness, and every time I puked, I prayed that it should not be what I suspect it to be. I told Aakash and he went to the nearest medical store and got us a pregnancy test kit, the results came out to be affirmative. I was so scared. We didn't know what to do. We couldn't risk going to the hospital due to the COVID situation and we weren't sure of the expenses. I spent the next few days taking emergency ipills but they didn't work obviously. So Aakash asked one of his friends and he suggested some other contraceptive. I took it's concentrated dose." She continued to narrate her horror in a detached sense.

"On the third day of taking the pills, I started to bleed. Oh Aaradhya...." She broke off crying.

".......it was so excruciating. It wasn't just the pain, but my own flesh and blood, my own foetus that I was losing, my unformed child. I am so condemned. Ever since this abortion, I haven't been myself at all. I feel so hollow. I feel like I've lost a piece of my soul. I lost motherhood. My heart aches at the sight of children. The guilt of having killed it compounds the grief." She continued, "Ours is a family of Hard core Hindu conformists. My dad is so orthodox, that if he or any of his brothers come to know of the act, I'll surely be dead. I can't stop feeling corrupt and immoral."

"Listen Vanshika I can't take away your burden, but I can only promise that the hurt will recede. Just don't try to force yourself into some sort of a repetitive haunt of what's right and what's not. You can always call me if you need to put down your thoughts." I say.

I am shocked at this sudden dump. The girl who wouldn't stop saying that sex is a form of meditative energy and one shouldn't share the body without a certainty about the relationship had taken such a drastic, life altering act and was probably going to live in a blame for a long time.

"I think you should go back home now. Tell your family that since there were some reported covid cases in the campus, you've decided to come home." I suggested, afraid that she might harm herself.

Long after the conversation was over, I spent an awful amount of time brooding over her trauma, feeling personally inflicted.

CHAPTER XVII

The Glass God

The mornings saw a breadth of expansive sunlight sheltering the sallow moor in its golden luxury. The effects of COVID had not penetrated the country life as tragically, and people still lived safely in the safe haven of their farmlands, their routines unaffected.

A few miles from our place was a local water catchment, its fringes scooped with silt from the runoff waters in seasonal streams during monsoons. Its picturesque composure extends serenity, a meditative calm, a placid perfection amongst the heated desert land. Baba used to bring me here occasionally.

This is where I learnt swimming as a kid. He had told me. My school wasn't as privileged as yours. We didn't have a fancy pool and an instructor. We learned by hit and trial on our own, clinging to those low branches of the peepul tree looming over the waters. His narrative power was so profound that I could almost picture his words, they filled me with an imaginative rapture of his childhood days and I could almost visualize his little figure floating and kicking on the waters with his brothers and school friends. His life though plain and simple used to enthral me over my own city life, consisting of comfort and convenience. I used to envy his crudely uncoached and free upbringing over my fabricated and carefully curtailed lifestyle.

I sat snuggled under the fierce shades of the peepul tree, the dense canopy bustling with thousands of birds in a thrilling discord. I counted and identified around seven bird sounds and the rest others were a new differentiation for me. I felt bridled by these twittering eruptions, my mind at ease. It almost felt like a patron figure was brooding over my melancholy, offering solace through a peaceful medley.

Here in the village my life felt largely spaced, like every single day underwent a variance of an unabridged gap before finally submitting into an outpour of a long starry night. Life was lowly yet peaceful, vacuous yet meaningful. The rhythm was almost slow but catchy. It was like living in a classic black and white movie, its tape caught up in a slow motion, repeat. The air were clean. There were no buildings punctuating the vision of a vast sky. It was like stretching indefinitely into an open space irrespective of how or where the origin lay. The only compunction that meddled my willingness to stay here indefinitely was a lack of network and poor internet connectivity, I'd barely attended any online classes here so far. My family members spoke Rajasthani and the subtle references to their folk songs and lore often lost their depths upon translation, almost alienating me from their true essence.

College campus life in a metro city was a haphazard rush where the days melted into nights in the blink of an eye. Even though I was surrounded by people my age, who spoke in the same language as I did, lived through the same trends, fast forwarded to modernity, globalization, technical rapidity of futuristic sciences, discussing politics and international affairs, religion and customs, engineering and architecture, coffee and sautéed dishes, sitcoms and romcoms, yet I felt alienated. I always felt split between these two worlds, born into one, brought up into another, but a participant in neither. I always felt like a ghost warping between two spaces simultaneously and I felt naked to the visibility and scrutiny of those around me. I felt like an animal who had lost her shell, each of my struggles to fit in at a camouflage being weirdly noticeable.

I fell asleep without a realization. The desert vapors collecting around me, and the sand particles condensed in the air, looking like a frozen scene from some science fiction film. A red haze emanating from the short cacti, the sun hung low, looking oblique in its solarity. A feeling of being very alone grappled my bones, the world was devoid of humans and humanity, and I was the lone survivor of this post-apocalyptic vision. I could distinctly hear sharp murmurs, recognizable as the familiar voices of my college classmates, but I couldn't see any of them. It felt like some invisible glass partition separated me from them. I was trapped in this small hollow cove of unending dunes, oblivious to the world beyond the glass walls. I saw a small shadow wavering horizontally, a few yards from me and as I traced its source, I saw Harshita. She looked like a dome-shaped, two-dimensional creature from Gulliver's Lilliput. She hadn't aged unlike me, looking exactly like a replica of her picture torn out of the class photograph. I turned away from her, sad and scared. My instincts told me that if I focused on the voices, I'd be able to snap out of there. Even though I kept reminding myself that it was just a dream, I couldn't stop the panic and tension building in my muscles. The more that I tried to focus on the sounds, the less intense they kept getting until they finally died down. Everything around me sublimated into a dense white fog and I saw my Nani walking through it, she turned to look at me, smiled, and floated away. I felt the isolation tighten around my chest, and my eyes fluttered open, even though my body lay limply paralyzed.

My thoughts palpitated as my heartbeats quickened. A sharp tangle of white daylight crashed into my eyes, falling through the peepul leaves in white brisk spots. I felt an unexplained ache for my earliest best friend Harshita, that turned into my longing for Baba. I sat there, de-energized, torn, and tortured from the aftereffects of the dream. My head felt like a tissue paper sap, sogged and clammy. The afternoon sunlight cascaded along the waters, piercing like crippling laughter on the ripples.

Baba's memories became a tangible missing, haunting and grappling my wake at the least expected moments. Here in the village, I had no mental engagement to keep me occupied and sane. The feelings that I hadn't made peace with, continued to replete my despair with pain. His death had been very sudden and unexpected, as is in the case of all kinds of accidents: he was here just a moment ago, and then in the very next minute, his existence was obliterated forever. Maa and I had gone to my school for an award ceremony for the rank holders in the matriculation exam. I had invited Baba to accompany us but he refused to take the day off. I knew that it was more because of his insecurities to adapt to the well-educated and groomed gentry of the crowd. I recalled a time in my second grade when Baba had come to attend the parents-teacher meeting and one of my classmates had made fun of his rural attire - a plain white kurta pajama and a safa. Even though he must've felt terrible, he persisted in wearing the same at all formal social gatherings, can't wear a three-piece and look like a Bollywood actor, I'd end up looking like an imposter, impersonating some business class ruffian. He had said.

On the tragic day, he had gone to the construction site - a multi-storied session court, a government building of significance. The quality of the cement and other construction materials used for the building was very substandard, exuding a threat of constant collapse into rubble even before its completion. Even though Baba and several others had highlighted the cause, the Civil Engineer and the Chief architect were far too busy making personal gains to have paid any heed to the advice. The heavy rains from the previous nights had dismantled a few pillars on the rooftop, and to prevent others from meeting the same fate and resulting in a disastrous collapse on a passerby below, the workers were instructed to uproot all of them. As they busied themselves with flinging out the pillars from the base, the shock sent a nearby slab into dislocation, without anyone's notice. The two children playing underneath would've been severely harmed had my father not leaped forward to barricade the slab with an iron rod lying nearby. His shout of alarm had made the kids run to safety and brought attention to the misshappening but it was too late for himself. He was flung below with a jerk, tumbling down, his body being pierced with the iron beams, killing him instantly even before crashing to the ground.

When Maa and I were told the details (much against our requests), we couldn't cry. We tried to numb ourselves. Our lives were fragmented forever, pushing us into a void surrounded closely by guilt and self-hate. Our thoughts mutilated our peace every day. Maa lived in a chain of only if I had accompanied him on-site that day, he would perhaps still be alive. While I was constantly incarcerated only if I had forced and begged him to come to the award ceremony, he would still be happy and alive.

The architect and the civil engineer got away with the blame by paying off for it. The government officials tried to write us a monetary compensation for his life insurance but Maa declined. She didn't want to sue the company and the associates involved because the entire process of laws, lawyers, and justice was far too netted and unjust, corroding your resources and energy until your last breath.

Money can not bring back the dead and we won't accept the benefits of his death. His life was worth more than what any of you scoundrels can value. She had said.

I trudged back, weighed down by this sudden dissociation and flashes of torment. It felt like a sudden funeral inside my head. Little did I know that I'd be suffering the same collapse upon reaching back home. Deep told me that Nani had passed away an hour ago. The family members and neighbors were gathered around her body wrapped in the customary shroud, on the verandah beside her cot, where I'd last seen her awake and alive.

She died peacefully Deep had whispered. It was probably due to the old age that despite having recovered from the illness, her immunity had withered.

Nani wasn't someone that I had spent a lot of time with. I only came to visit her during my school vacations. Whatever I remembered of her, was mostly an imposition of what I read in stories of grandparents like the portrait of a lady, overlapping the imagery and character of Kushwant Singh's grandmother as something of my own. I often attuned to what my mother told me about her own childhood days, trying to picture Nani. In my memories of her, I'd seen her as someone with a Rajasthani lehenga, wearing bangles made of ivory. Wrinkles folded on her face like crevices on a weathered mausoleum rock. She was a very pious lady, devoting maximum hours of her life to prayers. She was a woman of very few words but very affectionate gestures and blessings. She made me sit on her lap while she peeled water chestnuts and unwrapped coconut toffee for me. She fed and milked the cows, who felt soothed only by her touch and presence. The calves used to frolic around her in delight, their white marble bodies and kohl-lined dense eyes twinkling with tender innocence. Nani had an unspoken bond with the cattle of the farm.

During the winters, she would make mangodi, bari, bhujiya, rabori, and papad made up of chickpea and gram flour adequate with the perfect flavors of cinnamon, peppers, and other spices and pack them in large containers along with homemade ghee and send it for us. Maa would cook them and I would savour the sabzi with chapatis made of millets.

Ever since my Nana's death (grandfather), she had been an efficient matriarch, bounding the family effectively, until Mama took over the land and housing.

In the past few days, she had been like a fragile glass god, aging translucently. Even at such an ancient-looking age, she hadn't lost any of her memories or senses. But now she was a lost frailty passed into an abode of heavenly stature. I looked at my mother, bent over Nani's body paying her last religious dues, her eyes moist and her hands shaking. The sight burned my heart but I prevented myself from crying, walked ahead, and took my mother's head in my arms, allowing her to weep and crumble as I held her in a role reversal, caressing her head like she was my child now and not an orphan.

CHAPTER XVIII

A Disordered Fallacy

It had been two months since Nani's death. Maa had already busied herself with her teaching work in Jodhpur to avoid falling victim to the flashes of grief. It was my mother's most brutal and incomparable coping mechanism. I writhed away in pain and agitation succumbing to the most unproductive days, academics of rote online routine had been inadvertently pushed to a backdrop while the psychological imprisonment of the lockdown came to the forefront. I tried applying for online internships wherever I found vacancies, but the response was always either neutral or negative. I gave up, retreating to deal with myself rather than the world.

Vanshika and I started experimenting with online gaming, exploring platforms to distract ourselves from the eclipses of reality, and finding an easy escape from prolonged boredom. We spent the day working on false online accomplishments, levelling up in the games, and compensating for the losses in the real world. It earned us the needed validation, and assurance and made us feel better.

The Cyborg's Odyssey: An online simulation game where the protagonist levelled up, starting in a prehistoric Era with dinosaurs and mammoths, fighting the wreckage of these gigantic creatures before moving on to tougher levels of Renaissance treachery, leading troops in a cold war and ultimately fighting aliens as a cyborg. The game became progressively absorbing as it became more challenging and futuristic, surpassing every level. It was like living through evolution and history before traveling into an alternative hyperspace, thwarting enemy space shuttles from destroying life on Earth.

Persian Knight: The game that was initially launched as a classic version by UbiSoft for Nokia phones now penetrated the gaming market with an upgraded three-dimensional interface. We could live within a multiverse, where infinite choices led to infinite actions and storylines. The Knight had to save the golden city from being invaded by a foreign emperor and save a diamond shrine from being lost. With a successful completion of every level, your character becomes more upgraded with strength and weaponry to combat the enemies and save multiple lives. We felt nurtured by the savior complex, indestructible because even if we failed, we could begin again. Life was never lost and we could actually save people from death, unlike the suffocating reality of the real world outside.

The Mercenary's Saga: It was our favorite game. We could equip the central character with military aircrafts, personal choppers, customized bikes, tanks, and submarines. The weaponry was a rich collection of assault rifles, shotguns, DMFs, sniper rifles, SMGs, and other throwables. It was a team game where your performance depended on the Kills you bagged and the survival tactics you adopted. Vamshika and I used to spend hours plugged into our laptops and headphones, discussing strategies to win, shouting "Kill", and "Danger Ahead" into the microphones, reviving each other, and making it through the end. We also talked about our lives while playing, making dark jokes of disturbing sarcasm.

There were a few other games like chess and ludo that we played when we needed a passive break. The racing games allowed us to cruise control the vehicles while our own lives spiraled out of focus and domination. We found the games a purgatory bliss that let us cope with the faults in the offline life with an online aversion.

The days ate themselves up and the possibility of the restoration of normalcy felt like a far-fetched pursuit. We hollowed ourselves from the mock legendary conquests in gaming that no matter how addictive, were largely inefficient to make us forget about the daily depression. While my reflexes improved on screen, my body withered and became obese due to lack of exercise and stress eating. As we continued to suffer, killing zombies and fighting biological wars on our androids, the government too occupied with religious majoritarianism, political warfare, and fascist mudslinging continued to ignore the grievances of the affected populace. The doctors and the police forces tried to keep the surges of mass panic under control.

One day, Chrisanta, one of my old friends from school called me unexpectedly. She was hosting a low-key birthday party in her house and she invited me saying that the atmosphere would be completely safe and none of her family members and 5 other guests, classmates whom I knew had been infected. While I had intended to refuse due to my introversion mode, she had successfully convinced Maa to force me to accept. All the meals will be exclusively cooked by me at home. Sanitation is sanity. She giggled.

Maa said I needed fresh air and some real human company, the gaming addictions were making me lethargic and vicious and she wouldn't hear a NO for an answer. I had to submit.

On the day of the invite, I had emptied the contents of my suitcase, trying to pair the clothes that I could wear. None of the options felt wearable (not because I'm a girl) because I'd gained too much weight and most of the jeans didn't fit me right. Finally, I fished out an old pair of stone-colored denim jeans and a white kurta that I'd previously worn on Holi. It was drizzling outside, and the somber mood matched the inner dilemma. I let my hair down, half clutched them with a small banana clip. When I was ready, I checked myself in a mirror, instantly anguished by the image that I saw. I looked like the Penguin logo on the Penguin Books. I looked gloomy and not jaunty, also it could fit onto the spine of the books but I was too obese to fit anywhere. I cried and wanted to spend the day in bed. But Maa persuaded me to go and I vowed to start dieting and get myself on track as I hurried to Chrisanta's place.

Her house is a duplex, standing ostentatious and proud in Jodhpur's posh colony. As I rang her doorbell, fighting the urge to go back, Chrisanta appeared, wearing a bright pink jumpsuit.

"We've been waiting for you. Thought you weren't gonna show up because of the rain." She said, leading me upstairs to the living room hall.

Crap, everyone is already here which means I'll have to walk into a bunch of eyeballs gauging me. I'm so undressed. I'm so obtuse. Does my hair look okay? I thought in a sudden panic. As I entered, everyone broke into a greeting smile, nodding and waving all at once. The Vittoria cushioned sofas circled a custom decor sheesham wood table, the setting giving off the rich vibes of luxury. One of the walls was Adorned with a huge painting with a life-like depiction of Noah's Ark. The pair of animals were portrayed so realistically, that one could almost stay immersed in the genesis of the flood narrative for hours. On the adjacent wall, there was a picture of the life cycle and eternity of incarnations from Bhagavad Geeta, starting with a tiny baby, transcending all the human ages before finally growing into an old man, and then from his ashen skeleton rose a new baby. The chain erupts infinitely beyond, a symbol of rebirth and continuum. I vaguely recalled Chrisanta telling us about her parents being love-married from two different religions. Her name Chrisanta Shukla suddenly made sense.

"Oh my God! Darling, you've changed a lot." Falsha interrupted my chain of thoughts, with her greetings. "Where is the perfect girl, the grace model that we last saw in tenth grade?" She continued.

"Heard you are pursuing engineering?" Vidya spoke, shifting to make space for me on the sofa, inviting me to join.

I nodded meekly, smiling as I sat burying myself in the soft cushions, thoroughly conscious of my heavy weight.

Natasha and Saloni, seated beside me, were already engaged in a dispute over who's better: Gigi Hadid or Kendall Jenner.

We laughed and talked about the good old days and the pseudo-comic side of our missionary school lives.

"I remember how you used to recite the final prayer ten minutes before time upon our request. And the peon used to be so annoyed for having to ring the bell, marking the end early. Your voice over the intercom used to bring us so much peace as we felt happy for the school day getting over." Natasha said looking at me, I nodded in recollection.

"Remember the time when you, Saloni, and I sneaked into the restricted areas of the resident's quarters and found the Principal chilling with wine and pork?" Chrisanta laughed.

"Not to mention a week of suspended leave that followed. And the anger of our parents." I said, shaking jovially.

"Also, I always used to hate that all of your letters to my best friend were addressed to Vidya and Chrisanta but never me. That made me so jealous" Saloni said, wiping a fake tear from under her lashes before erupting into a genuine laughing fit.

I was having a great time. Even though all of us now lived in different cities for graduation, the time that we were sharing now felt more real, almost as if we had never lost touch. It was like visiting back the favorite events in your childhood but with the freedom and independence of an adult.

Chrisanta's birthday cake was a customized unicorn with vanilla icing, baked by her mother.

"Preservation of the child within." She said mimicking a horn on her head like a unicorn. We sang her the traditional happy birthday, as she cut the cake.

"It's mint mocha underlined," Saloni observed, tasting a mouthful of slices and rubbing the extra cream on Chrisanta's face and we all followed the cue in doing the same.

Chrisanta and her mother kept bringing us trays loaded with the most delicious food ever: Spicy chole bhature, saucy skillet lasagna, dumplings with cauliflower and mashed potato fillings with their thin membrane stretching into flavourful mixes, noodles and pizza garnished with paneer, cheese, bell pepper and zucchini, caramel infused donuts, homemade blueberry cheesecake and chocolate ice cream.

"You guys are the best cooks on the planet," Vidya said appreciatively, scooping a dumpling.

"Better than Gordon Ramsay or Sanjeev Kapoor," Falsha added.

"This is way better than what we could've ordered from a Cafe or a restaurant," I said.

"You're barely eating Aaru," Chrisanta said.

"Have more if you genuinely like the cooking." Her mother added, re filling my plate with lasagna.

"You eat too little for someone your size," Vidya said as she passed me another donut. "This one is a different flavor."

The remark, though meant as a favor, made me self-conscious.

After the dinner, we spent the rest of the time playing Truth-Dare-Situation, prying upon each other's secrecy and relationship status.

When I came home, Maa was already asleep. I covered her with a shawl and snuggled next to her, falling asleep immediately.

The next day, I received a carton of freshly baked cookies and chocolate sauce with a note that read - Thank you for gracing the birthday get-together with your invite. I loved your gift. Hope we stay connected. Delighted with the pleasure of your company, enjoy the cookies that I made for you. Loads of Love :)

-Signed, Chrisanta.

I smiled.

I accepted the following request of my friends to stay in touch with them virtually. But soon enough, I found myself falling into an unhealthy obsession with a perfect life, advertised by Instagram models and body influences. I drew unhealthy parameters for comparing myself with others even though I was very much aware that the virtual world was endorsed with a Fallacy, a facade of idealism. As I binge-scrolled through reels and stories, it kept occurring to me that I needed to get myself together, I needed to fix my routine. I followed a few profiles for a fit of inspiration. I started reading health blogs and food journals on the internet, criminalizing calories as the prime reason for being overweight. I started dieting, cutting down a few chapatis a day but there was no observable change and I felt defeated. I started skipping ropes and cutting down calories. Once or twice a month I went to the nearest clinic for a routine checkup and the results were astonishing, my weight had dropped considerably. I was an ideal 60kg now, perfect at my height. But the goodness that kickstarted me was also inspired by a desire to get control of my life and emotions. Social media still made me feel dissatisfied with the achievement as I compared myself to the perfect bodies no matter how unreal and unattainable it could've been. I continued to live a calorie deficit routine and the falling numbers on the scale and the measuring tape gave me a masochistic pleasure. I'd only heard of eating disorders like anorexia and bulimia, a Western psychological catastrophe, far too far to happen to someone like me living in a moderate household in India where all these were just textbook descriptions for courses in nutrition and physical education. I'd read about famous Hollywood actors living on the diet of "an apple a day" under the close supervision of the doctors. The idea seemed inviting to me and I thought nothing could go wrong, living on dangerously low food intake. I'd started to fit into my 9th grade dresses again and I felt more than happy, felt like an upgraded version of the video game character. But despite all this, the weight loss had been so sudden and drastic that I felt like I didn't own my body. It felt like I was living inside somebody's rented space. I didn't feel like me. My energy levels declined and by the end of the day, I felt overwhelmed and exhausted. I became obsessed with numbers, read food labels closely, monitored every bite I took, and ended up overestimating the required intake. But the physical exertion and adrenaline pumping made me feel better, I could fall asleep easily. Even though my nightmares deteriorated, with visions of my father being buried in the rubbles of some famous building, him dying by being crushed under a train. Harshita haunted me too, one time I saw her hanging from the ceiling, and the hands that had tied the rope around her neck were mine. I often woke up cold despite the heat and I hated myself for everything that had happened to my life. I'd started to get more and more depressed. I'd started to think that if I hadn't received good grades, I wouldn't even be awarded and my father would still be alive. I could feel Maa accusing me of the same even though the only fights that we ever had were based on me not eating enough. I remembered the calorie count of all the foods that I ate, my mind always calculating and converting volumes and kilograms to kilojoules and kilocalories. The more I obsessed, the more everything felt distant. Soon enough I started to want to disappear, I wanted to occupy as little space as possible, physically as well as mentally. My bones felt hollow and my darkness ossified.

Diwali came and went by, without me feeling happy and I avoided sweets even on the day of the festival. I'd sat in the corner, crying for Baba while Maa sulked in the kitchen, reflecting my dark mood swings. My classmates were spamming social media handles with tweets and posts that read, we came home for Holi and Diwali has passed. The ten months of Lockdown had become too much to handle. Starving myself felt good and eating felt like a sin. I used to fast until my blood sugar levels went down and I had to binge eat to make up for the depleted nutrients that eventually led to more guilt and suffering. Another March rolled by, and I felt fatigued with the cyclical repetition of the days.

CHAPTER XIX

Paradise Lost; Paradise Regained

By April end, the news that the college might reopen had begun to float. The vaccinations had started and even though there was a raging debate about its efficacy, it kickstarted a wave of optimism. Maa increased the student intake of her tuition classes while I had finally got an online project and busied myself with the research work, the intravenous time had slipped into a busy schedule for both of us. Even though there were days when I battled depression and the urge to give in, my new body and the project meetings gave me some sense of control over my life and the strength to continue to prevail.

Maa had overworked herself and started complaining of feeling weak and feverish. One night, she nearly collapsed, her temperature skyrocketing within hours. I started to panic but she asked for some mild antibiotics, promising she'd be better by morning. But her health worsened and she had to be hospitalized immediately. The doctors suspected COVID-19 and she was shifted into an isolation ward where no family members were allowed despite my urging and begging to let me be with her, they forced me into a quarantine in our home. I called Deep and he promised to come at the earliest.

The next day, Deep came with Maa's medical reports from the hospital. She had dengue and her platelet count had fallen drastically. She had been unconscious for the past ten hours and showed no symptoms of recovery. The news broke me completely. I sat frozen, unable to comprehend the sudden change of events.

"Listen, Aaradhya, take a grip over yourself. Maasi needs you as her strength. You can't give up already." Deep said, trying to talk me out of a stiffly blank state.

His words sounded so hollow and distant as my world crumbled and my insides screamed.

Why me? Why me? Why do the people I love keep leaving me? I kept thinking.

"Aaru, I'll take you to the hospital tomorrow morning. I've asked the superintendent in charge and he has been obliged to help us." Saying this Deep left to follow up on some medical formalities.

God, please I don't want to have yet another void stretching inside me. I don't want to keep dying this way. I can't live this way. I kept shuddering and praying, unable to stop my tears. Even the faintest possibility of her dying was too much to bear, I coiled on the bed, shaking like a child. Everything in the room reminded me of her, the shawl was still wrinkled and the cot dangling from her weight had carried a fair amount of her living imprint on it. Her green saree lay crumpled on the chair, I pulled it closer, burying my face in it, sniffing in her fragrance. I clung to it for emotional support.

Aaradhya is a very prodigious child, Sister. If you give her a chance she'd prove me right. She is very competent.

She'd requested for an entrance and interview from my School principal for admission. She'd bring me my lunch box in the interval so that I could eat my food while it was warm.

She would help me with my homework and indulge in playing hide-and-seek, seven stones, and ice water with me and my friends after school got over. I remembered her reading out Grimm Brothers fairy tales to me. The afternoons where we lunched peacefully, reading about her favorite movies: Mughal-E-Azam, Kajal, Kagaz ke phool, Joker, Shaheed. The Sunday columns featuring her favorite actors, and actresses, and the stories of their lives marked by ethical overtures, filled her with such pleasure and fondness. Qayamat Se Qayamat Tak was the first movie that she had watched in a theater soon after her marriage with my father. Your father had saved his earnings to take us to see the tragic romance movie. Even though he was not a big fan of the film culture, he loved me dearly to make space for the things I wanted.

I cried recalling the past few months arguing with her about meals. I wouldn't eat anything that she cooked and lived on oatmeal prepared in milk. What if she never cooks for me again? I shivered thinking. Rajma Chawal and Halwa were the last food items that I ate with her. I recalled it inadvertently. I shouldn't have broken her heart. Oh God, please bring her back to me, I promise I will be good. I kept saying it as a repeated repentance.

A million memories splintered like broken fragments of a mirror, stretching in minuscule of heightened emotional awareness. All these moments seemed like they were still occurring like they were not a part of the past. I wanted Maa to stay alive. I wanted to switch my breath for hers. I kept yearning for her embrace, the touch of her hand on my face, the caressing nourishment.

I took out a photograph from the album, Maa was holding me in her arms, her eyes shining with maternal affection as she looked dotingly at my baby form. I cried, missing her already. I wanted to run to her. I wanted her to come and comfort me like she did when things went wrong.

Only if Baba was here, only if he were still alive, he would know how to bring her back. I thought.

I must've passed out on the bed with her saree wrapped around my arms because when Deep woke me up at 11 the next morning, I had almost forgotten about the misery. I looked at him through my swollen eyelids, blurry with remembrance and recognition. I must've drifted into some dreamless slumber because my head still felt heavy.

"The hospital superintendent has allowed us a quick visit for half an hour. Hurry up, we've got to see Maasi. Also, she's recovered quite well since the night." Deep said, much to my relief.

My stomach churned at the sight of the hospital. The smell of the medicines, the acid-washed floors, the grim-looking patients, the odor of sickness, and the atmosphere of death and decay always sent my head into hyperventilation. I'd recall Baba's dead body in the morgue. The corpse has no living language to convey its morbidity, yet a residual dark wafts the demise of the living, a sign of an absolute finality - the wrenched sense of an illusionary aspect of the material world. The sight of the blood still sends me into shivering nightmares. I quickened my pace, almost running to the emergency room where Maa lay.

She opened her eyes, smiling weakly as we entered.

"I feel much better now, my blood count is coming back to normal." She said.

"Shush....I'm really mad at you." I said, sitting beside her on a chair.

"Here, we've brought you some fruits and light food. You need to eat food for the medicines to get adsorbed properly." I sat unwrapping the home foil, and placing the sandwiches and apple slices on a tray.

She ate in a grim silence. Looking vacantly at the food.

"I had such a strange dream last night. I thought I heard you crying, so I walked out of the room and the corridors were vacated, there wasn't a single living soul-stirring. It felt so real, that I was quite unnerved. The silence rang eerily through the air, I couldn't even hear my own footsteps as I walked. The only sound was that of your wailing. I tried to call out your name but couldn't. Right at the end of the corridor, there were three aged patients with their backs turned towards me and their faces in the wall. And just as I was about to call out for you again, I saw your father, faint and transparent, almost made up of air. He waved, gesturing me to turn around, urging me to go back. Though he didn't say a word, I knew he wanted to tell me that you needed me. Then I came back and lay on the bed. And I woke up this morning. I don't remember any of the in-between stretches. It feels like there's a missing blank and I woke up to life this morning." Maa said.

"There's an afterlife. Aaru's prayers saved you, and her baba brought you back from the dead" Deep said.

"Even though I don't believe in any of this, I'm glad to have you back Maa. I almost thought you'd die and then I'd be dead too." I said tearfully.

The doctors said that Maa would be discharged by tomorrow evening. She will have to take extra care. He advised us to get her vaccinated only after she had recovered completely.

"Aaru your Maa is quite a Saint. She married your father and kept loyal to him and his family despite the fact that everyone treated her badly. They said that she married him because she was impure and nobody else would take a characterless woman in their home as a wedded daughter-in-law. Even though she was more educated and capable than him she always kept humble and took the right decisions for the family. She married him even though he wasn't a match because your Mama had chosen him for her. She believed that her brother's choice was the word of God. Your baba held her in a lot of respect and wanted you to be bold and intelligent just like her. They never quarreled. Now when I look at your family, I just feel for you. I think that your parents should've been more accepted by their respective families. You and your mother hold so much potential to uplift the condition of the village children." Deep said.

"We will do our best Bhaiya to keep up the moral legacy and would be more than delighted to serve people."

"Yes Aaru, never forget your roots. The base of your family and the homeland." Deep said.

When Maa came back, I cooked and cleaned for her and prevented her from continuing teaching until she'd recovered. In the days that followed, I tried to be more grateful for the little things that I'd overlooked. I didn't want to be in a place where I'd have to lose things to know their true value. My peace lay in keeping her healthy and in harmony, no heaven can offer a delight without a mother's affection for her child.

CHAPTER XX

A Sign of Good Times

Aaradhya:

By mid-April the talks that our college was taking an autonomous decision to reopen with permission from the MHRD had started to take a rumored route, too far to be real. But a week later when we received an email to stay ready with the vaccination certificates for the first dose, our joys knew no bounds.

"Hey, you heard?" Abhijeet called me as soon as he read the mail.

"Yeah," I said I was a bit disappointed because this was the first time in 5 weeks that he'd decided to acknowledge my existence.

"I'm so excited. I'll reach a week before the said date." He said.

"Cool."

"Are you off? Do I sense dejection? Are you not happy? Did I do something wrong?" He asked in a quick succession of conscious statements.

"Five weeks too late to be checking in on me," I said.

"Aaru I swear I called you like six hundred times, but your calls never connected. I thought you were unwell because I didn't see you attend any of the online classes."

"Oh, yes. I was visiting my native village. Also, Maa had fallen sick, so...." I trailed off.

"Oh. I'm so sorry. How's she now?"

"Recovered and Rebooted," I added gleefully.

"I had a traumatizing breakup recently." He said.

"What the fuck?" I nearly screamed. "You've had a girlfriend and I've never known? When were you going to tell me?"

"You didn't know? I'm sorry, I thought everyone knew." Abhijeet said, trying to cover up for the mistake.

"Well, I didn't. So glad to know that the person that I believed was my friend had been keeping a secret all along."

"Aaradhya, that's not true. I thought I'd told you.... I mean I thought I'd shared how we'd met, the story of our first kiss, our first valentine, and everything.....it was a four-year-old relationship."

"Seriously Abhijeet?"

"Hey, I'm really sorry. I mean I've been such a big mouth and I thought everyone in the college knew."

"I'm a fool out here, living in a betrayal like it's normal. A friend keeps a secret that he'll be dropping out to join elsewhere and another one has been in love all along. Nobody seemingly wants to share what's been going on until they need me." I said crying and breaking down in anger.

He didn't say anything and I instantly regretted lashing out at him. "I'm sorry Abhijeet, I didn't mean to say all of this."

"It's okay, I've been a brunt of feminine rage lately." And he broke down in a laughing fit, telling in immaculate details of how his ex had started to experience a lack of attention in their long-distance relationship before she called it off. He tried to turn his heartbreak into some comic story, trying his best to shield tears behind laughter.

I'm not going to the US. Abhimanyu texted me one day. Lately, all the Instagram reels and memes that I'd been sending him about 'life abroad' were being left on read. He hadn't even responded to the last text that I'd sent him on WhatsApp. I thought I was being ghosted.

Why??

My Visa got rejected due to the COVID thing and all :(

Oh, I'm so sorry. Feel bad for you.

Nvm. I'll have to continue college.

Sucks, I know!

Yeah. Gotta make up for a lot. I've run too far behind on the academy! Besides, cg runs low at 6.32

You'll make up bud!

Siddhartha packs his bag, nervously fumbling through his articles, weighing the necessity of things before placing them in. He intends to stay away from home as long as possible. The hostel seems like a good getaway plan. The past few months had been a suffocating nightmare for him. Sejal had died and he couldn't stop blaming himself for her actions. His Dad had become so morose that he beat his mother even more frequently. Siddhartha intervened as many times as he could, physically exerting his dominance over his father. But the situation had started to make him temperamental with bouts of uncontrollable aggressive fits. He'd been undergoing therapy for a month now and the meds haven't been helping him cope noticeably. He quickly placed the pills in a small corner in the trolley bag, without his mother's notice. He couldn't afford to let either of his parents become aware of his mental health.

"I'm sorry Sid. I should've been a better Mom to her." Mrs. Sharma said.

Siddhartha had stopped speaking to her entirely.

"Can't you stay a little longer? What would I do when you're gone too." She said sadly.

"I can't stand being here anymore and even if it were possible to delay the departure, I wouldn't do it. Besides, don't lament me going, I'm not dead unlike her." Siddhartha said hateful.

"You've become like your dad. You're exactly like him." Mrs. Sharma said, shaking in fury.

Siddhartha stared at her in shock, unable to digest her words of wrath.

I am nothing like him. I don't want to be anything like him. I hate that he is my father. Siddhartha thought as he stormed out of the house without turning for a goodbye.

Siddhartha sat staring out of the train window, the speed slowing his thoughts. The noises of people on the train silenced his inner voice. It won't get any better. He thought to himself. But it won't get any worse either.

As the distance between Dehradun and himself kept increasing, it felt like he was getting out of the chains of some dark captivity. He'd been trying to drag himself out of the abysmal quicksand that was acting as a suction of his life. At Least Sejal might be having some peace now. It felt like he switched her place, living in the void that she'd previously inhabited.

We need to meet. We need to end things in person, as mature people do.

Siddhartha had left Kiran's text on read for two days. Finally, he decided to text back, anxiety made his fingers shiver.

Ok.

Blue ticks flashed instantly and Kiran typed back as if she'd been waiting for him all along.

Let's meet when you come back to the campus.

Ok.

Kiran was in final year now, coming to write down her end-semester exams while Siddhartha still had 2 years to suffer through graduation.

The memories of Kiran overpowered him. The hurt was as fresh as it had happened just a couple of minutes back. Why do people always end their relationships in the places that they have had the most memories in? He thought to himself as he visualized a break-up kiss under the Kachnar tree of their favorite secluded spot

Post Lockdown

CHAPTER XXI

The finite elements

The campus premises looked hauntingly unreal, inviting, and frightening at the same time. We'd been allotted single rooms and I unpacked my stuff and was arranging the books when my phone rang. It was Abhimanyu.

"Hey!"

"I'm back," I said ecstatically

"Please, let's meet immediately."

"Give me 10"

"See you at the back gate?"

"Cool"

I walked to the back gate where Abhimanyu was standing, immersed completely in his phone. My heart fluttered in a daze. I've never seen someone look more precisely perfect than he did, like some sort of a model street styling; a denim blue checkered shirt with brown cotrise shorts, his hair longer than the last time I'd seen, falling down his neck in perfect curls. He had gained muscles and weight, looking well-built and athletic. He stood tall, his fingers typing on the screen of his Android at lightning speed. As I came closer, he looked past me and then back at me, his face breaking into a recognizable smile.

"Oh God, no way." He said

"What?" I asked, stupefied by the brilliance of his face.

"You're...skinnier?" He stuttered.

"Yeah, I mean....." I said, looking down at myself consciously, and shrugged.

We stood there gaping at each other awkwardly and for the first time, it dawned on me that neither of us knew how to give or take a compliment. I extended my arm for a handshake, his fingers clasped around mine, cold and clammy just like I'd remembered.

"You smell nice." He said, inching closer, carefully putting a strand of loose hair behind my ears and stroking my ear lobe with his thumb. I shivered at the close vicinity of his figure, his face at an excitingly close distance, for a moment I thought he'd kiss me, but then I stepped back scared and conscious.

"Thanks."

"Kaafka's Palace?" He asked.

"Let's just order in instead? I have been wanting to take a walk around the campus."

"Sure. Cool."

We turned back towards the road leading to the intersection of the hostels and the central lawn.

The breeze was balmy with nocturnal blooms of the moonflowers, the scent luscious and invigorating. Bougainvillea fluttered in the shades of white pink and orange against the backdrop of a greying sky. The petrichor lifted off the earth like a nested breath, it'd been drizzling all day and the streetlights and the lampposts glowered in the rippling depths of the small pools of water.

"So what's the lockdown been like?" Abhimanyu asked.

"Umm.... A Lot."

"I know, right?" He said, sounding distant and fazed. "The world won't be the same place again."

"Yes."

"So....well....I learned to drive and also procured a license."

"Wow. Let's be off to some place cool, soon"

"Sure."

"I've undertaken a project under one of the profs from the college itself. The work is super cool."

"Wowzzyy....tell me more."

"Umm....it's some sort of a simulation work on finite elements analysis; in a layman's language the prototype testing for the vulnerabilities in the mathematical model of a proposed engineering design. We write some partial differential equations and test them against a set of constants and parameters for their accuracy."

"I should've taken chemical too. Sounds dope."

"Well...."

"The vaccine is a sham," Abhimanyu commented. "The conspiracy theorists have been suggesting that the after-effects of the dose would make us go blind and zombiefy everyone. The vaccine is deadlier than the virus."

"No way Abhi. Do you wanna be endorsing some indigenous herb, instead? Like some Patanjali kind of made-in-India product?" I asked, rolling my eyes.

"Totally. Some sort of a shamanic spiritual medicine, rather....."

I laughed.

"No, I'm dead serious." He insisted. "You won't believe me, they were checking the bags and screening our pockets and I completely forgot that I had a rolling paper and a lighter on me."

"What....?"

"Yeah. Insane."

"They just let you go?"

"What else would they have done? I wasn't carrying any psychotrope. That would've landed me in any legal trouble. One of the guards stared at me like he wanted to make a cannibalistic lunge at my lungs but he had to suffice with confiscating the paper and the lighter and with a this is not what your parents have sent you here for. Little did he know I'm practically an orphan." Abhimanyu said darkly.

"I'm sorry, what?"

"My mother and sister died due to COVID."

"I am so sorry...." I stammered, lacking words for a condoling comfort.

"Well, it was pretty awful. My mom was in the isolation ward for more than a week and they cremated her body without letting us have a last look. Sadhya caught it after 3 days. Though I'm pretty sure she died due to emotional insufficiency and not the virus....but.... anyway.... I have lost all the family I had." He said, his voice devoid of emotions.

The sullen darkness shadowing his disposition suddenly made sense. It was like falling into an unending rabbit hole. I could almost sense goosebumps breaking through my skin, erupting as empathy.

Later that night Abhimanyu called again.

"Hey, I wanna date you. And I wouldn't mind if you said a NO. I'd still be the same." He said in a single monotone.

I'd always liked Abhimanyu, magnetically levitating towards his erudition and musical charm. He was the kind of guy that always fit my definition of physical attraction. It took me several minutes to register that he was actually asking me out. The guy that I liked for all these months actually liked me back.

"Are you high?" I asked, my words slipping out of my mouth like they were a system-coded audio and not something that I had a cursory control over.

"Yup. Soaring."

"Well when you get down, ask me again," I said, trying not to sound eager.

"Well....if you say so."

My heart thrummed with a restless energy throughout the night. I kept missing the smell of his perfume and the lavish black curls.

The next day, we sat on a bench on the central lawn. He kept switching songs, playing uke and humming; low down rolling stone, fill in the Blanks, November Rain, everlong.

"Hey, I am sober, and what do you say now?" He said strumming, playing, that a broken heart is blind.

"Yes."

He looked up smiling, blushing. He leaned in, his lips brushing against mine, his intoxicating, probably cannabis infused bleu de chanel exuding a masculine citrus smell. He kissed me, moving his mouth softly around mine. I shuddered, whimpering softly, kissing him back unrestrained.

"What?" Abhijeet was what-ing me for nearly a millionth time now. He was the first and the only person that I told delightedly (much to his complete shock and horror) that I was dating Abhimanyu.

"Since when?" His vanilla ice cream melted out of his bowl.

"Ordering a vanilla family pack was a very bad idea," I said, scooping the melt from the edge.

"No. Hang on. Do not deviate from the topic.

So here I am, looking at you after almost a year, you've not only changed your physical personality but have also lost your heads. And you're dating Abhimanyu?" He said staring, his eyebrows corrugated in a disbelief conjecture.

"Yeah," I said, smiling shy and sly.

"Well.....good life." He said, raising the bowl to his lips, drinking the ice cream melt. "Why didn't you tell me before?" He asked, aiming the empty bowl at a dustbin nearby.

"Because he asked me out yesterday only," I said dipping my French fries in the residual vanilla melt in my bowl.

He looked at me with contempt, "You're getting weirder."

"Can we normalize mixing flavors for a pre-menstruation craving? I said, offering him the vanilla French fries.

"Don't you think you rushed?" He said. "Oh God, this is awful." He spat out the fries.

"I mean, I know my heart."

"Too early for the Heat to run into an erroneous calamity." He said, making a shooting arrow, cupid style.

The college lectures came back into a routine and even though the subjects were just as unbearable as they'd been previously, yet the sight of the board and classmates gave some sense of comfort.

"Everyone has been talking about you," Abhijeet muttered under his breath during a mass transfer lecture.

"About what?"

"Just things. It's like everyone in the college knows you for some apparent reason and I'm the only one who sees you as a new stranger."

The teacher hushed us and we couldn't continue the conversation.

"Hey, I wanted you to meet Atharva," Abhimanyu said, introducing me to a senior.

"We know each other already," Atharva said.

"Oh yes. Thats right. The Literary Society head." I nodded in agreement.

"You've changed so much Aaradhya. Working on some cool novel, yet?"

"Nope. I mean lockdown was a total waste and now I'm stuck on a project."

We went to the back gate where Abhi and Atharva smoked and talked about CSE lectures and professors.

"Hope we are not boring you to death?" Abhi said, putting his arms around my shoulder and kissing my forehead.

"Not at all," I said

"Ah, she's already retreated into the imaginative corners of her thoughts," Atharva added.

CHAPTER XXII

Everything Perfect In The Coffin City

There's something tragically poetic about falling in love, and I'd always been positive that none of the lovers' sickness would infest me. But here I was, every day, every minute falling so deeply, so deep, that my life started to gravitate around Abhimanyu. The forlorn sights and the monotonous routine of the campus had somehow started to feel bearable. There was a certain meaning to the day, a looking forward kind of positivity.

Data procurement is carefully subjected to the reactant concentration, contact time, temperature, and reaction rate. Kindly ensure that the plots are drawn accurately in origin and apply Wei-Prater analysis for the complex reaction network....... The lab and lecture instructions of the professors became a slow background hum while I performed calculations and procedures absent-mindedly. The hands that held the pen, scribbling notes and performing complex mathematical operations belonged to a mind flooded with a lover's oxytocin high. Abhijeet would often snap me out of daydreaming into some sort of a judgment bias. My brain chemistry changed every day while my heart sang Lana del Rey:

They say that the world was built for two

Only worth living if somebody loves you.

Abhimanyu would be waiting for me outside the labs and lectures whenever he got over earlier.

"We should've been in the same department." We had said this over an infinite number of times to each other. I was always texting him while we were away and when we were together (which is most of the time) we spent all the time being the cringey love birds that both of us had evilly despised earlier. Back in our rooms we would video call each other, ranting about the Academics, discussing movies, banned books over history, absurd conspiracy theories, psychedelics, music, and a post-COVID reality. Every day we discover something new about each other. He spoke obsessively and reverently about Julius Irving, Kobe Bryant, Bill Russel, and LeBron James, following their game tricks and talent. We played basketball together and the evenings left us cherished.

On the weekends we drove to the city outskirts, trekking and exploring the nearby towns and old forts. The village - Motigaon, almost 30 miles from the main city was our usual hanging out spot. The local legend said that two centuries back, the village was an epicenter of the British Activity, the local rule had aligned with the foreign interests and collectivized a lot of trading at the heart of the town. The people lived with prosperity and dignity until one of the neighboring kings invaded the territory and the harmony capsized into violence and chaos. The natives started committing suicides and there were unexplained cases of mass hysteria where women exploded into violent fits of dancing and dying, setting themselves on the flames. The village quickly turned into a burial ground and has been a cursed haunt of said and believed paranormal activities. The story, however thrilling, had been a source of dismay to us; we never encountered a ghost despite our treading and frequent ventures. The place attracted us because it was situated on a slightly raised land and the trekking spots nearby gave very scenic views of the cities below.

Atharva, Abhimanyu, and I went to the city outskirts as usual one day. Atharva drove the rental car while Abhi and I sat in the backseat, vibing to the music, looking at the scenes blurring past.

We discovered a ruinous cemetery outside a huge dilapidated city. It was our first time in this area. The Graves with names like James Murray, Alexander Rebello, Elizabeth Bedley, Cassandra Simon, Andrew Williams, and numerous others dating to the colonial era, lay scattered around. The place, remote and downcast with a sorrowful aura, made us feel a little gloomy too. Abhimanyu and Atharva sat down on a wall of the haveli, with their backs pressed against a pillar while I looked around the tombs circling between tamarind trees and passion flowers, being pulled into a time long gone by with only a withered stagnation left in its place. It started to drizzle, making the atmosphere serenely suppressing. They decided to roll a joint.

"We certainly live in conformist times. Acting like more civilized beings, rule-bound and moral." Atharva said, crushing the cannabis buds.

"Yeah," Abhi said gruffly.

"I'd say we have more liberty than we had previously," I said.

"Nope. Free will doesn't exist. I mean you'd like to think it does but it doesn't actually. Just think of the decisions you're allowed to make for yourself." Atharva said.

"We do have our independent choices that are not a function of some social parameter. For instance, you're free to vote and elect your representatives. I'm not saying that majoritarianism doesn't come into play, but at least you have a say in political and constitutional decision making unlike the countries run by dictators or the politically and socially unstable Islamic states." I said.

"Well, that is just one side of the scenario. First of all the rule of majority is influenced by propaganda and those capable of accessing control over resources. It's all about how people can be brainwashed and herded like cattle. People living in unstable dictatorial or one-party socialist governments would barely know the difference between their living and that of the rest of the world. We are very conformist people, adhering to what is acceptable, be it the law of the state or the family. Do you think that you can ever let go of the emotional ties or the relationship obligations to the people that you are bound to?"

"I mean, why confirm? Why not resist?" Abhimanyu said, rolling the filter paper.

"Why would you resist? I don't see people armed in a rebellion until they are brainwashed into believing that their ideologies should clash with what you're blindly served with?". Atharva said.

"War perpetuates necessity. It adds meaning. Time and again you need to rise and suggest that idealism can be restored. I would want to believe in cultish idiosyncrasies. If something feels right to you, you should make a go for it." Abhijeet said, lighting the joint and inhaling a deep puff. He grazed up, his head supported on the shoulders looked like a limp crescent disc, his chin angled at the sky. "Waging wars to establish new ideas should be the rule..... Aaru you need to try this stuff. I'm entering paradise." Abhimanyu chuckled.

"And then meet Rodion's fate in the crime and punishment?" Atharva said, disagreeing.

Atharva passed the joint to me, I looked at it with a bit of resistance and uncertainty.

"Here" Abhimanyu put the joint between his fingers and inhaled, showing me how to do it. "Make sure that the flavored cold stings your throat while you take it in through the whistle like a gap between your teeth. Hold it in for a while and then exhale."

I did as he had instructed but nothing happened. I had felt a sharp sensation in my throat while taking the cannabis-infused air but nothing happened. Maybe I haven't done it right. I thought and took in two more quick and deep puffs before passing it to Abhimanyu again.

"Abhi, it's not working. Am I not supposed to feel dizzy?" I asked. He looked down at the joint completely stoned, his pupils contact while his irises swam in brilliant colors, his eyes red as a rose.

"God I'm high," I said as the color of his irises swam around his face and floated through his hair, I saw him dissolving into swirling colors of bright pink, green, and yellow. I looked around shaking my head, frenzied with laughter. The rain fell around us in small circular droplets and I experienced "time dilation" in its virginal form. The drops elongated and became squishy gel balls as they hit the soil, bursting into colors. The leafless tree skeletons changed into color-filled sap of brown and white extensions.

The world turned into a happy little swarm entrapped into blessed coffins. I felt like a bird as free as could be, soaring, contemplating, living. Free will exists and wars are victories too. Every element seemed utterly laughable as happy hormones encroached on the brain.

I lost track of time, living between a happy dreamy state, and my phone rang with a shrill. Atharva was passed out on the wall, his body twisted like that of a snake. While Abhi was staring at the sandstone, his head was on my lap.

The caller displayed Abbijeet's name. I answered, "Hullo?"

"Where the hell are you?" He asked, sounding out of breath and urgent.

"Umm....somewhere in the skies below the cotton candy clouds," I said.

"It's no time for jokes, Aaradhya. Please put your sarcasm aside. This is my seventh call. Prof. VP Patel has been trying to reach you."

"What, why?" I asked, surprised, trying to jostle myself into the grip of reality. But my head felt like a water-filled balloon.

"Who is it?" Abhimanyu asked, his eyes crescent in a trance state, grazing my face in reverse mode.

"Abhijeet," I said.

"Yes?" Abhijeet answered the phone.

"No. Not you. I've been telling Abhimanyu that I'm talking to you." I said to Abhijeet over the phone.

"Why does Prof. Patel want to see you?" Abhijeet asked curiously.

"I'm working on a project under him. I had a meeting at 4.00 and I forgot to bring my PC." I said.

"Hmm," Abhijeet said before he cut the call.

"Strange world," I said, slipping back into oblivion.

A loud rustling startled us. We looked around confused, the darkness had fallen into a warning concavity.

"Ghosts?" Atharva said, chuckling chilly.

"The souls' unrest," Abhi said.

"Let's not disturb the calm of the dead world," I said, my stomach rumbling loudly with hunger. "Food," I complained.

"I'm famished too," Abhijeet said.

"Come on guys, I know a place." Atharva started up in a lead.

As we were trudging through the wilderness, the trees and the bushes opaque against the proposed solidity of the dusky sky, all three of us stopped dead in our tracks, frozen in horror. Glaring at us was a pair of iridescent eyes flashing like neon lasers.

"Coyote?" Atharva broke in fright.

"No. It should be a blue bull." I said.

"It's gotta be the aliens," Abhimanyu said.

"Run, this is no time to waste on debates like this." I shrieked and all three of us made a blind run for our lives, scratching our skin against the thorny branches impeding past our motion.

"This way!" Atharva screamed, pointing at our car.

I looked behind, tunneling close at our necks with a foul breath and a blood-curdling snarl was some indescribable wild beast. My body paralyzed with horror, Abhimanyu yanked my hand, pulling me into the car and I looked at him horrified, having lost count and consciousness for a few minutes.

"That was pretty close," Abhimanyu said once we were bolted safely inside the cars.

"What the fuck was it?" I asked, still hungover from the frightening sight.

"Werewolf." Atharva giggled, looking at us in the rearview mirror.

"Haha, very funny," I said, annoyed.

"To be honest, I didn't see anything," Atharva said.

"I just heard a roar," Abhimanyu said.

"We are high," I said, settling the argument with a definitive statement.

Atharva braked at the entrance gate to some posh colony, asking for the details of an address from the gatekeeper. He parked the car and we walked into the colony, the people doing their little routine tasks: walking their dogs, the aroma of dinner emanating from the kitchen, couples watching television, kids going back after a play in the safe space of their homes. The coziness of living spaces like this filled me with a sharp longing for home. I need to call Maa. I thought achingly.

Atharva guided us to a lift of a nearly 17-storeyed building. The elevators weren't working, so we took the stairs, huffing and cursing at every floor.

"How much more?" Abhimanyu complained, clutching his stomach.

"He lives on the 13th floor," Atharva said, casually.

"What the fuck." I said.

We were in the living room of a common friend of Abhimanyu and Atharva - Siri was a school senior of theirs. The short guy, with a very angular and square build, was already high when he invited us in.

"Munchies" Atharva quackery in an imitation, gesturing hunger.

"We are baked and were haunted by some coyote-like creature..... where's the kitchen," Abhijeet said, rising.

"Right to entrance," Siri said.

The four of us stood around the stove, assembling utensils and edibles.

"You live in a landfill," Atharva commented, trying to find Chilli powder.

"You're welcome, fellow pig inhabitant," Siri said, spanking Atharva's butt.

"Gay. Very gay." Abhimanyu laughed.

"What about this?" Siri said, kissing Abhimanyu's cheek.

"My girlfriend would mind," Abhi said.

"Girlfriend?" Siri turned around to look at me like I was a sudden apparition in space between them and had never existed before.

"Unbelievable right?" Atharva asked.

"Yeah. A Raccoon like you with a goddess like her?" Siri said.

"Now, now. Don't flatter him too much. Lest he starts to infest the area with self-importance at his game." Atharva said, breaking into a high-pitched laughter.

We made mushroom curry, creamy and flavourful. Everyone's appetite had become so gigantic post-weed that we had eaten up 2 packets of the multigrain bread in 10 minutes but were still hungry.

"Let's order a pizza," Atharva suggested.

As Siri and Atharva quarreled over chicken pepperoni and farmhouse pizza, Abhimanyu led me back to the living room and we sat down to choose between the options of games to play.

I suggested Wanderer's Desert Quest and beat him by a score of 114-79. Atharva chose the Racing Rapido next and I beat his motorized robot by a very close 3-2. The night rolled with food, fun, and unending dope.

CHAPTER XXIII

Surging Strands of Sadism

Aaradhya:

"Where have you been?" Abhijeet asked as I came to the class five minutes late. He'd saved a seat for me next to him.

"Was dropping Abhi to his DSA class. The room number had been changed at the last moment." I said, almost yawning and trying to bury my face behind my hands.

"No. Where have you been for the past two days?" He said, rolling his eyes.

"Motigaon," I said, trying to suppress yet another yawn.

Plasticizers are low molecular weight, liquid or solid substances that are added to the polymers to enhance their softness, plasticity, and flexibility. Now if you consider two different gases with different concentrations, separated by a thin polymeric membrane.......

I tried to follow the words in the class but my mind was still hung over and sleep-deprived from the ventures of the day before. I gazed out of the window, the soft breeze laden with a shimmer of cold, made the Indian laburnums and golden trumpets host a distracting golden delicacy. The Glass windows were still foggy and rain droplets trickled down their surface in a condensing race, making the scenes outside look like an oil painting.

"Can you be more specific?" Abhijeet demanded, breaking me from the visual imagery.

"I was with Atharva and Abhi. We'd trekked for a while, got Stoned, and then went to visit a common friend of theirs. Fun day." I said drowsily.

"Wait, what? You've been doing drugs?" He screeched loudly, earning us a contemptuous look from the professor. I sat in complete silence thereafter, refusing to oblige the queries that he wrote on a piece of paper in my notebook. He even gestured for me to get online but I refused.

"Don't wanna take the next class. I'm still on a trip and I need coffee to wake me up." I stood up complaining after the lecture was over.

"Yeah cool, let's go to the canteen."

"I don't know what you've been thinking but I don't feel you're in your right head," Abhijeet said, dipping his samosa in the chutney.

"I'm fine....." I said, covering my mouth as another yawn broke involuntarily.

"You've stopped taking your project seriously. You take more of the CSE lectures than your own. You spend an awful amount of time at the computer center, God knows doing what. And the most disturbing thing of all, you've started to be a completely different person. The girl who's never smoked or has ever drunk any form of alcohol has straight up plunged into all of them."

"Just a little bit of change in routine. I'm just experimenting and it's cool. And besides, everything is fair in love and war."

"Kiran, we really need to stop seeing each other," Siddhartha said.

"Don't tell me that you don't feel for me anymore." She replied, caressing his hair fondly.

When he didn't say anything, she pulled him closer and kissed him.

"Does it not feel the same?" She asked, her breath and lips moving around his mouth. Siddhartha felt a pulsating rage course through his body, he pushed her away a little aggressively.

"This is exactly how you kiss him too. Isn't it?" He was disgusted with himself and her.

"Siddhartha, I'm sorry. And I'm saying this for a millionth time now." She said, turning away from him.

"Yeah, and it doesn't fix anything. It doesn't make a wrong into a right. I came here to break up with you in person. Because you wanted me to look you in the eye while doing it."

"Yeah," She turned around, rising on her toes. "Do it. Tell me it's over." She offered.

Siddhartha looked at her feeling the strength drain out of his body, all the stolidity leaving his expressions. He pulled her closer, nearly lifting her off the ground, and kissed her again.

The moon hung like a paper circle with rusted fringes, the brittle yellows sinking in towards the center. Abhimanyu and I sat under a dish antennae on the rooftop of Dronacharya hostel. Boys and Girls have a separate hostel and my action of foolish audacity could lead me into serious trouble. But weed sobers down every anxiety and thoughtful perception into a long rope terminating into some nihilistic pothole. Abhi lit a cigarette and passed it to me after a few puffs.

"My mom hated my dad." He said looking into the black distance, outlined with whitish light around the undulating slopes of the hills.

"They were having a bad marriage before he died. And I remember her yelling You are so acidic that you eat up those around you. Your life, your very act of being alive is killing me. I don't know how much of it she meant, but my dad died just one day later. It was an accident, his car slammed into a wall and his blood alcohol levels were quite high. And my mom could never stop hurting herself over it. She'd sleepwalk into the house saying, she didn't mean it. I practically ran off to Kota to be able to study in peace."

"Sounds dark."

"Yeah. And just like that the entirety of my life exploded."

The smooth emptiness carved itself out, bursting into a grim demise. Abhimanyu cradled his head in my arms with his hands around my waist. I shuddered as his steel collar bones nudged my flesh. He looked up and sighed, pushing his lips on mine, the tenderness breaking like cherry dews on my tongue. His hands moved over my skin, his fingers tickling around my thighs like icicles on fire. My breath grew heavy, his curls darkened as the starlights above mushroomed into a tinkering twinkle. I kissed him back with a resisting temptation, torn between an urge equally frightening to participate and run away.

Our bodies long for sins even when our minds impose a control. The psychologists might have taken emphatic stands to suggest that the superego would do anything to establish individualistic control, but here I was, tumbling into faults and follies recklessly.

I sneaked into my hostel after climbing a not-so-difficult brick wall between the two hostels. The last difficulty of a second barrier was overcome by sliding from under the steel gates and I was inside the premises of the Girls hostel. I looked around and saw Nivedita(one of the CSE students in the same year) staring at me baffled.

"Tell no one," I spoke and walked to my room.

"I've been hearing indecent things, which I strongly believe are rumors in your name," Vanshika said, while we were standing in the mess line, waiting to load our plates with the inedible mess food.

"Let's go to the canteen. They're serving mashed potatoes again." I said putting my plate back and turning to leave.

"What rumours though?" I asked as we'd placed our order.

"Some nasty stuff." And she winked.

"Yeah. Why do you think they're rumors?" I said, laughing.

"So it's true?"

"Guess so."

Aakash had asked me to meet him, the pleading in his voice pressed with urgency.

"You must know already?" He asked.

I looked at him confused.

"About our abortion." He said.

"Oh, yes. Right. Yes. I mean very unfortunate."

"I mean I know it was my fault but it's wrong of her to punish me to this extent." He said, his eyes brimming with puppy innocence.

"From what she's told me, it doesn't look like your fault completely."

"It is in a way. I was the one who insisted that we move in together. I didn't wanna be without her even for a day." He looked almost tearful. "Whatever happened should've never happened. But I miss her. Can't she at least talk to me? Am I so hideous now? The other day she saw me sitting right here and she walked past, giving me an intensely loathsome look. It's nightmarish to even think that the person that you are ready to be with for the rest of your life is torn away from you, the person that you love so dearly ends up hating you."

I heard murmurs and gossip about myself. Most of them were about a girl who had spent a night in the boys hostel. People were indulging in some very disturbing graphic talks. Even those who didn't know me stopped by to stare.

"Everyone seems to know," I told Abhimanyu.

"I didn't tell anyone, just Atharva that too because he wanted weed and I told him that you and I had smoked all of it the night before in the hostel."

"Nivedita from your branch saw me sneak back into my hostel. But I highly doubt her to be the origin of these rumors."

"Nah. She's far too busy being a nerd. She's got no friends to talk to." Abhi said.

Abhijeet yanked me back by pulling my lab coat after the excruciating 3-hour work practical was over.

"What?" I asked furiously.

"We need to talk."

"Abhijeet, I know already. I know they are talking."

"So, you're OK with it all?"

"Why would I care?"

"You need to see this. Weren't you scared?" Vanshika said, handing me her phone.

I looked at the picture, it was that of Abhi and I kissing. The background of the hostel rooftop was easily identifiable.

"Where'd you get this?" I asked, surprised. "As far as I know it was a timed selfie in Abhi's phone."

"Yeah, well everyone has access to this and everyone knows the girl who dared to be in the boys hostel in the middle of the night."

"What?"

"Abhi we need to talk."

"Yes?" Abhi said, sounding high and bored over the phone.

"It's about our picture. It's been circulated through WhatsApp media. Would you tell me how?"

"I'll find out. It's no big deal. Don't you worry?" He said and hung up.

For me, intimacy was about feelings and not about lust. I felt bad at my character being questioned and my identity being objectified. I called Abhijeet, crying.

"Well, you knew this all along," I said.

"Yes. And you can't accuse me, I tried talking to you multiple times." He said.

"What do I do now?"

"I think you need to talk to Abhimanyu. He should not have sent the pictures afloat and said things that he did."

"He doesn't have a clue either."

"Aaru he's the one who started it."

"No, it can't be."

Abhi, how could you? I texted him.

Take it easy. It's no big deal. Couples kiss all the time.

That's not what bothers me.

What is it then?

Why does everyone know? Atharva told me that you're the one who showed him the pictures. He even exaggerated that you were showing off to the other guys that you had a chick pulled out and had the best night of your life.

Well, I am really sorry. I was lust bound and I didn't think much.

It's over, I'm breaking up with you.

Aaradhya, you can't. I was just lust bound but now I feel for you. You can't just leave me.

CHAPTER XXIV

Rain Wrenched

The rains splattered across the window panes and the thunders lashed the skies. I sat in the room curled up to drive away the cold, waiting for the hailstones to stop splitting my ears. My phone had been lying discharged and I hadn't even bothered plugging in the charger. I lay stiff as a stone, my heart hammering against my chest, frenzied with laments and curses.

I remembered watching it rain in the school, the grounds flooding into puddles. A friend had once told me that if you'd stare at the ripples for long enough, you would be able to see dead people dissolving away. That's how you say goodbye to your friends. She wrote Harshita's name on a chit and gave it to me, asking me to float the tiny piece of paper in the water. This would stop the nightmares she'd said confidently. As we watched the ink dissolve and the paper pieces sog and sink to the bottom, I felt regulated. Almost as if someone had decided to lift a heavy weight from my chest. The nightmares never stopped but I began to be less frightened of them. I stopped being scared when Harshita appeared in them. I knew I had sent her to the waves where she could lie amongst her favorite fishes someday. I wanted to keep living in a place where the dead weren't constantly dragging me down. Breaking up and betrayal had been a sudden calamity. The very person whose voice notes and practice audios I'd saved in a

Playlist to listen to whenever I felt hunted down had now become a source of great distress.

"Aaradhya, let's just say that even if the things that he's been saying about you are true, it's still wrong on his part to give away the personal details and intrude on your privacy like that. It's an unacceptable behavior, and trust me you did the right thing by breaking up." Abhijeet had said.

But even hours and hours of crying brought no relief. I could go on talking about the hurt, try and fix things but it didn't justify the ache. I was going insane with guilt and grief. Thoughts and feelings ran about in loops of constant repetitions.

"Aaradhya, I'm sorry. Just give me a chance and I'll fix it." Abhimanyu said after I went to see him at the central lawn.

"I'm not here to get things better. I've just come here to know, why?"

"I didn't know that things would take a turn like this."

"Yeah, well I kept trusting you and you kept wasting away my faith in you. I loved you, Abhi. Is that what I'm being punished for? Everywhere that I go, people look at me a certain way. I hear things about myself. Things that aren't true. Things that shouldn't have left the privacy of our intimate lives. You made some sort of a fucked up spectacle out of it."

"Aaradhya, we've barely dated for two months, it's too early to think that you're in love. Just give me a chance,

I'll erase the dark parts in our story."

The loud disc music fragmented in the club. The dazzling lights dimmed and intensified in a dizzying rapidity. Atharva brought me a glass of vodka.

"Coke or soda?" He asked.

"Neat. " I said half emptying the quarter-filled borosil glass.

"I never got to know your side of the story, though," Atharva said, passing me a joint.

"There's nothing to it."

The monsoons have a very twisted sense of humor. I'd spend the day thinking that I could move on with the hurt and then the waters would lash and tell me otherwise. Not a moment passed when I was not thinking of Abhi and the time with him. Every word and every moment burned like a caustic chemical. I missed his company and conversations. I missed touching and kissing him. I missed waiting on and for him. I missed holding his hand. Every place that we'd been to had an essence of us, a part that we'd left behind unintentionally. Every memory stayed frozen in its place while I was being forced to move on. I would wake up with a hungry longing for him, fall into a vacancy through his absence, and sink into a gloom without his embrace.

Too early to be in love. Too early to be too much in love.

I hated myself every single day. No matter what my friends said to comfort my decisions or whatever new gossip that the campus buzzed with, I was always tormented at what exactly had gone so wrong in such a short period.

A relationship should never fail to mean something. Even years after it's gone, it should be able to move you to feel some type of way.

I was left with his words. His half-bred promises and his full-fledged lies.

We look better when we are together, identical. Almost reflectional.

And now I hated myself so much that the face in the mirror didn't look like it belonged to me.

How can one stay sober all their lives?

I was trying to pawn the sobriety with intoxication that made me black out.

It gets better with time. Wounds heal. They would say, while I lay watching the cuts bleed even more so every day. It'd been a month since we broke up and I'd spent the majority of time lying in bed.

"You're running low on attendance marginally in two subjects." Vanshika had informed. But I barely had the strength to register the repercussions. I'd tried postponing the project meetings before finally calling it off.

"You're not going to miss the exams or apply for medical," Abhijeet said, calling me the night before the mass transfer examination.

"I haven't studied. I'm barely in a state to understand a word." I said resigned.

"Okay, let's do it together. Even I'm starting just now."

End semesters came and went by without an impact. Usually, I'd labor for hours to submit my assignments, study for the tests, and keep up at a decent pace but this semester went by like all of my life was not my own, like my life was happening to someone else and I was a detached being, watching my own life like a nonparticipant, distant observer.

How are you? I'd texted Abhi when one of his branch mates told me that he hadn't appeared for a single test.

Fine.

He texted back an hour later and I felt relieved.

Atharva asked me to meet him at the central lawn.

"Are you sure you wanna continue with the break-up?" He asked.

"Yes," I said, even though a part of me wanted us to be back together.

"Well, ok. I'll ask him to keep away from you. Take care."

A week rolled by, and Abhi had neither texted nor called. I sat on the terrace with Vanshika. She had managed to sneak in vodka in a water bottle and we got drunk, smoking and playing music by ourselves.

I get home and there's a love note waiting

But only he is here tonight

And the words, the promises you're making

Only echo all these lies

"I am almost done," Vanshika said after 6 shots.

"OK. I'll do the rest."

"Do you think I should get back? I've been very mean to him."

"Aakash misses you a lot, Vanshika. And I don't know if you knew it or not but he left his seat in IIT to be with you."

I woke up drenched in sweat, the smell of liquor solidified the air in my room. I stood up, feeling sick and nauseous.

17 missed calls. After multiple attempts, I managed to unlock the phone.

All the calls were that of Abhimanyu. I called back, my heart assuming the worst of everything. He didn't answer.

Hey! I'm sorry, I just saw your calls. I texted, correcting the typos took me longer.

Nvm! Omw to Motigaon. Thought you might wanna drop acid.

No.

Cool.

The wait seemed to stretch on forever and the only thing that I hated about this waiting was not knowing what exactly was I waiting for. I felt hollow inside, like a part of me had grown into a void and I would never be able to become myself again.

I woke up feeling heavy with fright. I hated leaving my room if I was not heavily drugged. Every place, classroom, and laboratory was reeking of his memories. Every face that I saw was looking at me in a judgemental way. Maybe it was not as bad as it looked or maybe it was rotten beyond imagination.

The results were announced and I'd barely managed to pass in all the subjects, hitting the lowest for the first time. Atharva would often come to try and offer me a shoulder to lean on. But I mostly relied on him for a continuous supply of cannabis.

You deserve better. He'd keep insisting.

Aakash and Vanshika were back together and had eagerly adopted me. I'd spend my time third-wheeling, drinking, and bunking the lectures.

"They say, you're screwing Atharva now," Vanshika said, putting cumin seeds and garlic in the pan with bubbling oil. The smell instantly breaks down into an appetizing air.

"What does it matter? The damage is already done. Half the college has slut shamed me in their own ways." I said handing her the chilli and tomato paste grind.

I'd barely eat when alone. My dropping weight made Vanshika intrude on my melancholy by cooking food for ourselves in my room.

"You can't give up on food." She said.

"It tastes amazing."

CHAPTER XXV

Premonitions

Aaradhya

Some problems in heat transfer have an analogy in mass transfer. If the quantities and parameters are designated properly, the differential equations and the boundary conditions for the two would be identical......

The transport phenomena class was in full swing, and it was my first time attending the lecture. I tried focusing on what was being taught. The professor, a stout, middle-aged man, was teaching some sort of a derivation for heat conduction in a wire with an electrical heat source. None of the assumptions were made clear and I couldn't understand a word beyond the chapter's heading. The teacher went on with his drab, fidgeting a lot with his hands and jerking his head in violent nods. It rather looked as if he was trying to get his theoretical understanding to be delivered in a spurt of wisdom gurgling down his brain.

The board was scrawled with unorganized marker scratches, depicting some mathematical form of heat flux and expressions for maximum and average temperature rise. I tried to follow along but couldn't even discern the sequence of the solutions.

The guy right in front of my seat sat doodling laboriously. I couldn't help myself from sneaking a peak.

It was a caricature of the professor with transport phenomena equations coming out of his dead, his nose was extra circular and large almost like the whorls on a snail's shell. The thought bubble over his mouth read, "Engineering-a perverse lacuna. I'd rather bore you with prescriptions of mathematical scriptures".

Another one of those, I thought. Another one of those privileged kids who believe that they should be handed down the world just because they are too fragile to handle the freight of complex realities.

The professor decided to come take a look at our copies. The guy in front immediately turned the page of his notebook and began copying from the board, pretending to take down notes.

"Where are your notes?" The professor asked, standing beside my seat.

"I have been trying to follow directly from the board and the book," I said meekly, not meeting his eyes.

"Oh yes, lady? Do you think that you're so sharp that you can work the problems out all in your head without taking the trouble of picking up a pen and paper? Do you think I'm a fool wasting time here, junking away my energy on students like you?"

I felt a stab of humiliation rise in my bones.

"If that's how you continue, you'll surely fail my class." He said and strode off to the podium to continue his procedural deliverance. I was annoyed at being picked and pointed out when the cartoonist had got away safely.

The transport phenomena laboratory was a large hall with bubble cap distillation columns, heat exchangers, fluidized bed reactors, and gas absorption sieve plate apparatus hulking over the floors and slabs like an engineering warehouse from centuries ago. Half of the equipment was not in a functioning mode and the other half was so uncalibrated and obsolete that the results obtained were far too contaminated to make logical sense. We bent our heads, pulling roughly at our lab coats, murmuring exaggeratedly about how the experiments that we stood performing would do us no good.

"The results are incorrect. The graph is expected to be linear. This won't work." The lab teacher hissed angrily. "Experiment again."

Looking at the invalid data and output, the teacher decided to put us into a group of four. I was assigned tasks with the cartoonist, Rajneesh, and Vanshika as my lab partners.

After standing nearly for an hour against the thermocouple apparatus, jotting down variations, we sat down tired.

"I'll write the experiment." The cartoonist offered.

"I'll do the calculations," Vanshika said.

Rajneesh and I were left to perform the calculations.

My head had really suffered from walking along the dusty-looking fjord-like array of equipment and glassware. I hadn't eaten meals since morning and I could sense my blood sugar levels dropping. I sat shivering, typing the equation into the numerical for a failed hundredth time. Vanshika sensed my mood disorder.

"Hey!" She pressed her hand gently on my arm. "Let's take a break?" She offered condescending.

"What's the matter?" She asked while I leaned over the basin in the washroom, splashing water on my face.

"It's nothing," I said.

"Come on now. It's so obviously evident. Even Siddhartha was looking at you and was wondering and worried. Don't think of yourself as some sort of an invisible vapor."

"Who is Siddhartha? The cartoonist?"

"Cartoonist? I am talking about our lab partner."

We walked back in 10 minutes later. The sheets have been submitted and signed. The teacher called out our names, handing us each a set of instructions for the next class.

The afternoon sun gushed its flames, setting the tar on the roads in a blanching scorch. I walked, dangling a bag on one shoulder and holding an umbrella in the other hand.

"The heat waves," Vanshika complained, walking next to me.

The petroleum engineering lab was my least favorite of all. The professor spoke with an inaudible sonority and made such witless remarks and told the tales of his bravery that passing away the time with a literary anchorage was my only hope for survival. I immersed myself in reading on my phone. The experiments were usually easier and were finished in about 20 minutes.

The only unbearable part was breathing in the rancid smell of Sulphur Diesel and Coke.

"Aaradhya" I looked up when an unfamiliar voice called out my name. The cartoonist (Siddhartha) was extending his hand, "Give me your sheet. I want to copy the theory of the aniline point experiment of the last class."

I handed him the sheet and went back to reading. Siddhartha's face looked familiar but I couldn't remember seeing him.

Siddhartha, Rajneesh, Vanshika, and I became acquainted quite well. The conversations flowed easily, developing a comic relief from an otherwise tragic engineering drudgeries. We acknowledged brief moments of a lost longing for something unknown.

"It's the philosophical undertaking of an engineer," Vanshika said. "Wanting to be elsewhere and when the elsewhere were arrived at, not wanting the elsewhere anymore."

"Strictly mathematically speaking," Rajneesh said laughing.

Siddhartha handed us a cartoon depicting ourselves with a warning, "Choose life, not engineering."

I would often get a premonition that I'd subside as an anxious over-thinking. If I ever crossed roads and saw Abhimanyu, I would freeze. All the breath was knocked out of me. I'd heard several rumors of him dating again. I'd feel sorry for placing my trust in the wrong individual.

"Let's eat South Indian today," Vanshika said, scrolling through the swiggy while we were in the petroleum lab.

"Ladies, I'd like to accompany you," Siddhartha said.

"As long as you agree to pay, we're cool," Vanshika said, smiling.

"No way. I'm a hardcore feminist who doesn't believe in splitting bills. I'd rather have a working, independent woman be my sugar mommy."

Vanshika and Siddhartha were still fighting when we entered the South Indian Cafe.

Siddhartha and I decided to share a Mysore masala dosa while Vanshika ordered a medu vada for herself.

"So, what music do you listen to?" Siddhartha asked, tearing the crepe neatly and scooping the coconut chutney.

"Mostly rock and some metal these days."

"Ughhh..metal?" He said rolling his eyes in a judgemental way.

"Yeah. I like it because it's loud and cathartic." I said sipping sambar.

"I think that metalheads are violently insane."

"That's a rather biased projection," Vanshika said. "Aaradhya is too soft."

We ended the brunch with a filter coffee, the sweet and bitter yet refreshing vapors emanating from the tiny bronze mugs made the dining endurable. I caught Siddhartha looking at me and I smiled back.

"Is it really true?" He asked.

Oh God. Everyone knows. And everyone wants to know more.

"What?"

"You dated Abhimanyu?"

"Yeah"

"God, the guy is an asshole and I always thought that his girlfriend would be just like him but on the contrary you're not even close to what he is."

"What does that even mean?" I asked. The topic of my ex still triggered me even though it'd been nearly six months. I was overcome by a scavenging sensitivity every time anyone mentioned his name.

"Well, he's a junkie and has 3 backlogs."

"So?"

"You're just the opposite."

"That's an assumption."

"You drink?"

"Occasionally."

Abhijeet caught up after the evening lectures, running out of breath after me.

"Hey!" He shouted.

I stopped and turned around, dropping myself in his tender hug.

"How're you?" He asked.

"Good."

"Let's go out for a smoke. Please."

A while later the two of us were sitting outside a smoke bar when I saw Abhimanyu and Atharva walking in our direction. He filmed a casual Hi what's up to Abhijeet, ignoring my presence all the while. Atharva tried to offer me his cigarette but I declined. When they'd gone in, Abhijeet considered my state. I was stiff and morbid, unable to keep my legs from shaking and the tears fumed down my eyes.

"Hey, Hey it's okay." He said, wrapping his arms around my shoulders. I jerked his hand away, apologized, and walked off.

I hated myself that even after all these months, I was still in the same place while Abhimanyu appeared normal and fine. As is supposed to happen in situations like these, my hurt seemed larger to me than it must actually have been.

CHAPTER XXVI

Homecoming

The final year came as a relieving welcome. I was happy for two reasons: The first was that college would come to an end and so would the trauma. Second, I'd finally be able to take a break to do the things that I most liked i.e., pursue higher studies abroad.

Additionally, we were allowed to choose electives as per our choice, which meant that the engineering drag was finally over. As I submitted the priority order of my preference, I wildly hoped that Abhimanyu would not be in the same courses as me. I didn't have the energy to look at him, fondling his new girlfriend in the class. I was somewhat sure that we were not like-minded enough to land in the probability zone of the same subjects.

Even though they say that you should never let a wrong become a right, I knew my heart would chase all the wrong decisions until its very destruction.

I'd begun to spend a lot of time with Siddhartha. He had been a compassionate and patient listener. Though he would mostly just juggle around my lows and turn the pain into some sort of dark humor, I still found it a lot better to cope when I was with him.

Had somebody told me that it was possible to feel again, I would've never believed it. I'd lost all of my heart and soul to Abhimanyu. Even after he was gone, I'd readily emptied myself to the hurt as if he'd come back to me someday and things would be the same again. But the heart is always passionate about the terror lurking in the unknown territories.

Siddhartha was a person of melancholic disposition, an introvert with tragic depths. A forlorn vacancy set like a hardened rock in his manners. At times he would go sullen and solemn, like shielding some abysmal tragedies in his heart and when not sad, he'd be extremely vocal, cracking jokes. The traits that attracted me the most were his gentlemanly attributes and sketches (a subtle reminder of Abhimanyu). His voice was attenuated and soft at times, like some sort of a broken melody. He was shorter than Abhimanyu but had some matching features.

When the heart loses someone or something, it tries to cope with the loss by looking for the missing pieces in someone else, and the person who closely resembles the missing piece quickly becomes the link to fix things again.

The natural rhythm attunes us to find some positives in negatives. And some negatives in all the positives. Just like every human, I was swimming in a swarm of these rights vs wrongs; goods vs bads. Ever since my break up, the trust issues I've had with people just widened. A sense of abandonment took its place.

Siddhartha sent me an audio of two black holes colliding, the sound waves sonicating in a ripple so deep; for a moment it looked like the universe lived in its translation, even though life patterns wouldn't make any sense yet somehow, a fundamental longing; the Longing for love; to not be alone resonated in its space-time fabrication.

We were sharing cosmology lectures; learning about relativity and big-bang, and spending the evenings together. It felt like I was living in a repetition-a deja vu. If we ever trailed along my favorite spots, I'd be inadvertently reminded of Abhimanyu's hurt. His last words were a residual hurt marring my emotional capacity.

Siddhartha asked me out on a date and I said yes. We decided to keep it leveled, no strings-attached kind of theory. I never considered myself modern enough to believe in any of these modern-day relationship slang, I lived in an Era of some romantic idealism, neither too Victorian, nor very classic, but something more powerful. Yet when Siddhartha said that our relationship doesn't have a future, I agreed, suppressed my budding feelings, and diverted them as casual. But still being with Siddhartha felt a lot like home, like I was safe and rooted.

It's difficult to hide behind a mask when deep down you know you're willing to sacrifice yourself for the person that you are with.

I've always known myself to be an extremist- either nothing or everything. The intermediary normals have never suited the chaotic roars of my brain.

Siddhartha and I decided to go on a trip to Mumbai. It was an unplanned spontaneous spree, very impulsive but fun.

We sat near the Marine Bay, eating cotton candy, watching the waves froth and shatter and crash.

"I could stay here forever," I said, watching the sunlight tremble through its last brilliance.

Siddhartha leaned in and kissed me gently.

"Life looks enormously worth living when I'm with you." He said and I shuddered.

We strolled along the alleys in the old city, resplendent with vintage vibes.

"This is going to be my favorite street of all time, ever," I said, screeching excitedly. We entered a record bar, the underground shop had a variety of vinyls and albums, CD and cassette collections.

I saw several of Metallica's and my mind instantly said Abhi would have loved this. I edged back from the counter, urging Siddhartha to leave.

"What's the matter? I thought you loved music and such things" He asked as we stood sweating outside the shop.

"I do. But I still think of him. And it hurts. I don't love him or want him back but the fact that I still contain remains of such reminders of him just breaks me apart." I sobbed.

On our way back, Siddhartha sat perched in an aggressively foul mood and wouldn't talk or even look at me.

"I don't like to suffer from silent treatments," I said.

"You're still hung up on him. And you think I need to be cool with it?"

"I'm not hung up on him. I am still hurt and always will be."

Siddhartha curled up next to me, his arms around my waist. The sun streams pouring on his face made him shine like a golden god, like a marigold. He opened his eyes, his lips breaking into a smile, and his tongue searched my face in urgent whispers. I reciprocated the kisses.

"I love you." He said.

I stared at him, dumbfounded, pulling away from him.

"I really do." He insisted as he rose from the bed, pulling on his shirt. As he brushed and dressed, I looked at his tender habits that had so long formed a routine. Siddhartha liked his tea with less sugar and more cream. He was a sort of perfectionist and a cultured and orderly person. I reciprocated his feelings, trying to reflect on him. Even though I'd sworn that I'd never love somebody else, I was gripped with a feeling ardently powerful enough.

Siddhartha was an artist and had a large following of admirers on social media. But he used a different name and left no photographic identity around. It was as if art brought him life and death in equal amounts. His anonymous fame impressed me.

"Are you working on something these days?" I asked.

"Yeah." He said, coming closer.

"What?"

"You." He said pulling my bathrobe.

Our short film, the color ochre had been selected for television at a state-level event. Aakash, Vanshika, and I decided to make some quick edits to the screenplay and the cinematography.

"You're late again," Siddhartha complained as I went to see him at our usual place.

"I'm really sorry." I apologized. "Been busy with some editing work. You know how it can get."

"You could've told me to not wait."

It was the placement season and the final year students were at the peak of their career-related anxiety. A lot of software companies didn't allow for the chemical engineers to sit in the recruitment and most of the students who had lost interest in the core began shifting towards profiles related to data analysis and other managerial or bank jobs.

"What are you planning to do?" Siddhartha had asked me.

"Higher studies."

"Can't you just reconsider? If you take up a job here, we might end up in the same city and it would be good for our relationship."

"Siddhartha, I'll think about it. But I really feel that I need a push right now. I'm so perplexed."

I was walking to the lecture hall with Siddhartha when I saw Abhimanyu with his new girlfriend for the first time. They were holding hands and walked past us. I didn't feel as scared and nervous as I used to.

"You're moving on too," Siddhartha said, wrapping his arms around my shoulder.

CHAPTER XXVII

The Fractured Characters

I haven't been in touch with my first year roommates, friends from the other branches, and the seniors who had graduated. Life moves on and one can not stop the moment in time and continue looking back. In Abhijeet's words, life is unidirectional; it moves forward and not backward. Despite being the funniest person, he sat tormented with his ex-girlfriend slipping in and out of his life at her convenience. We'd spend some time together, studying for the tests. Vanshika and Aakash had taken a lot of care, to nurture my emotions as well as hunger post-breakup with Abhimanyu. I'd increasingly become anxious that soon all of my social circles would come to an end. Switching over to a new university, in an entirely new country might bring challenges.

Diwali was around the corner, students were going back home for a week. I offered Siddhartha to accompany me to Jodhpur.

"Maa would love to meet you. She likes all of my friends and cooks nice food for them." I said.

"And your father?"

"He's dead."

"I'm sorry."

"Will you come?"

"I will."

"I should warn you though, I'm not even half as rich as you are, on the contrary, I'm the poorest in your social circle."

"You better be kidding." And he laughed.

On the day before Diwali, Siddhartha and I got off at the bus station. Maa had been anxiously scrubbing the whole house despite me telling her to take it lightly. I called her to say that we'd drop in at the Bikaner Mishthan Bhandar and meet my school friends before coming home.

Chrisanta had been waiting for us with her boyfriend Pradeep. She'd insisted that we needed a double date.

"Hi," Chrisanta said, hugging me and Siddhartha. We reciprocated with smiles and handshakes.

"We brought you a little gift," I said, placing a pendant encased in a tiny wooden box in her hand. "We'd been to Mumbai and it attracted Siddhartha's eye, I told him this is something that you might love. It has a central turquoise colored sea shell."

"OMG. So thoughtful." She said, blushing.

We'd ordered a variety: Rasmalai, Dal halwa, Chhole Bhature, Pav Bhaji, Chocolate barfi, and a mango special Lassi.

"God this is awesome. This is better than what we eat at the Haldiram's." Siddhartha said, plunging deep into the Rasmalai.

"Guys we've got some news to announce," Chrisanta said after a while, showing off a ring on her finger.

"We've committed to be engaged," Pradeep said, kissing her cheeks.

"Congrats folks," I said, mildly surprised.

"It's officially been 3 years and we really love each other," Chrisanta announced proudly.

"Besides, I'll be completing CA final year soon and her parents have agreed to accept me. Haven't they, Darling?" Pradeep said.

"Oh yes, they have. And Mumma has already been hoarding the precious jewels that I'll be inheriting."

They kissed and hugged.

"The bill is on us, please." Siddhartha insisted. "Oh no. We'll do the honors." Chrisanta said, flirtatiously picking out the bill from Siddhartha's hand. "You can treat us when we come to see you in your college."

"Did I sense a red flag in their relationship?" Siddhartha asked.

"Hmm.....let me see. Well, Chrisanta is a Swiftie, so that's one."

"Pradeep has yet to clear his exam and their marriage might depend on his success. That's another."

"Gotta say, that's true."

Maa was waiting for us when we came. She nearly ran into my arms, excited like a child. The house had been tidied up, looking more habitable though largely empty. The smell of halwa and poori wafted through the atmosphere, exuding the presence of a loving warmth.

Siddhartha studied the place curiously, looking around the scanty objects scattered on the walls and hangers and tables.

"Told you," I whispered.

"I love it. It is humble indeed and yet so paradise-like. Almost a temple-like calm. It contradicts your personality completely though." He said.

"How do you mean?"

"You look fit in the filthy rich, the English speaking fluently classy chicks."

"Well.....I've been funded and brought up in a mission school."

On Diwali, Maa lit nearly 100 diyas. Siddhartha and I sat, adorning the verandah with a Rangoli, carefully crafting the outlines and pouring colors.

"Would you like kheer or ksheera?" Maa asked Siddhartha.

"What is ksheera?" He asked confused.

"Halwa, you silly I said. It's made of semolina, ghee, milk, and sugar and garnished with basil leaves and pomegranate arils along with the usual nuts and cardamom. It's served with banana on religious occasions."

"Wow. Yes, I'd love that. My mother cooks something like the sort too."

"You should call her," I said reminding encouragingly.

"Later." He said in a brusque manner and busied himself with the rangoli again.

Maa packed coconut ladoos, milk fudge and the ksheera in containers and handed them to us.

"Hope you come back soon and bring him along." She said while dropping us off at the bus stand.

"I will." I said.

Later in the bus, Siddhartha said that my mother really loved me.

"Well, I know. All mothers do." I said, beaming.

"Yeah. What was your baba like?"

"Nice." I said.

"Did he love you?"

"A lot."

"Why is love not reciprocal?" Abhijeet complained, downing a tumbler of whiskey. His eyes red, burning like bell paper on his vacant face.

We'd been discussing his breakup for a week now.

"She cheated on you. She manipulated you. How's that fair?" I said figuratively. "I'm not saying she's a bad person, but she's been doing bad things to you."

"I know Aaradhya. But love isn't so easy to categorise. It doesn't let you differentiate a wrong from a right. It is the most selfish yet somehow unconditional emotion. I wanna be out of this state so bad Aaru."

"You're committing the same mistakes that I once did. I thought you'd be smarter." I spoke, suddenly being reminded of a vicious loop of self blame and black outs. I'd tried erasing my life.

Later one night, Siddhartha, Vanshika, Aakash and I sneaked on the top of a water tank (Vanshika was drunk high and insisted we replicate the Veeru scene from Sholay but here we were, on some sort of an enactment from the three idiots.)

"I've never faced a disco (disciplinary committee) action. It's been on the wishlist for quite some time now." Aakash said, smoking a cigarette.

"Neither have I. But I do not even want to." I slurred.

"God forbid, I would absolutely hate it." Siddhartha said, his expressions of discomfort evident on his face.

"Cow. I bet you hate our company." Vanshika said to Siddhartha, peeling the home foil wrap off a burger that we'd bought two hours ago from a food stall.

"No I don't." He insisted, trying to fit in with us.

"You do. Because you don't even drink. How are you guys even compatible?" Vanshika said.

"I love him for being the sober man that he is." I said, putting my hand through his arm. "One of us needs to be rational and normal."

Siddhartha pulled himself away from me, looking disgruntled and offended at being picked.

This is what I hated the most about him, his silent treatments and talking through actions. I disliked it when he talked through his fists, his temperament getting the better of him.

As we grow older, we are supposed to get wiser but love pushes one in the throes of foolish behaviours and blind faith. When the sentimentality of the soul begins to float, the rationality of the head sinks. The final years calls for calculations and career planning, but here I was, trying to orient myself with the needs of my lover. Our arguments increased dramatically, making us a brunt of each others anger and hurt.

"Do you love me or not?" Siddhartha shouted over the phone.

"Of course I do."

"Do you think it's too much to ask for your company then?"

"Siddhartha, I've been giving ourselves a lot of time and my friendships have started to lose its mantle. I'd like to keep it balanced."

"I've never been much liberal when it came to reading Manga over Anime, obviously I love the later." Aakash said, while we were discussing Anime.

"I wouldn't know much about any, not a fan for real. Just read about the stories of the famous ones like the death note and the perfect blue."

"You should really watch more of them, they are pretty nice."

"I can't humanize them enough, hence find them very unrelatable." I said, refilling our glasses with vodka.

"I'm very much intrigued by Japanese onomatopoeia. They have the largest in the dictionary and even follow the sensory phonetics." Aakash said.

"Oh God, I thought I was the only one noticing such weird things because I was losing my head. Yes of course, I'd want for the Webster to make our dictionaries more inclusive. I mean some music are more fluid than the rest. If you listen to glass animals, really close you'd know what I mean." I said.

"Yes, like glass shattering, tinkers tinkling under water." Vanshika added.

"Exactly. There's more that create a similar auditory awakening; Mr. Kitty, Goth Babe, Childish Gambino, Slenderbodies " I said, excited.

"Eveb some R&B like that of UMI have a similar effect."

"It's 8.30 PM Aaradhya. Seriously?" Siddhartha complained.

"I told you I'd be drinking with Vanshika and Aakash."

"You've been with them for five hours."

"Haven't been calculating." I said irritated.

"Sometimes I think you'd like me more if I were a drinker and smoker and cool like you people."

"I'd never want to you lose your individuality to ascertain my feelings for you. There's absolutely no reason for you to compare. I like you for you and would never want you to be someone else."

Our compatibility issues had taken quite a rise recently, I saw ourselves drifting apart on the spectrum of understanding.

CHAPTER XXVIII

Denial

Siddhartha lay on the bed, staring at the ceiling. Kiran lay sleeping next to him, her arms flailing around her naked body. Her hair was frail around her face. The rhythmic heaving of her chest and breath sounded like an exasperated time ticking away, interlocked like a fatigued fate.

The night of the Mussoorie hotel came rushing back to his memory. Is this how Dad felt?

The guilty pleasure makes him sink into self-loathing. The room developed into a breeding ground of orgastic sin. The moonlight splashed through the windows, burning everything in the room with its guilty opalescence. The darkness outside the windows condensed like an impure filth.

"Hey," I said, rising to kiss Siddhartha as he came to meet me after the class.

He gave a quick peck and withdrew.

"How was the day?" I asked.

"Mom called. She was mad at me for not coming home for the Diwali." He said.

"I told you, you should've gone."

"With Sejal dead. Nope. Not a chance. Besides, not gonna lie, I can't stand my dad. We hate each other."

"Siddhartha I understand, but running away from the only blood bond you have serves no purpose. You can never change the family you're born into."

"Easier for you to say because you don't know what it's like to be in mine." He said aggressively.

"Kiran, we need to stop seeing each other. I have a girlfriend I love her." Siddhartha said over the phone to Kiran.

"Oh yes. And I'm no one to you? How are you different than me? How are you better than me?

"Kiran, stop," Siddhartha shouted.

"What for? You are a hypocrite. You think you have a way with the world. You think you have the right to fuck someone's feelings and be ok?"

"You have no right to tell me so."

Siddhartha sat, sketching on his canvas in his room, outlining the depiction of a woman tumbling out of a flower, blood pouring out of her waist. For some reason, he was unable to complete the facial expressions of the woman. He didn't seem to comprehend her emotions, and the thoughts perplexed him. It'd never happened to him before. His art was the only thing that he could root for, with certainty. It was the only thing in his life that he was confident about.

Kiran called him. He answered angered, "What is it now?"

"You need to meet me to break up." She said.

"Enough of this, Kiran." He sighed.

"You said you loved me. And you know no one else can love you the way that I do." She whispered.

"Oh yeah? You cheated on me." Siddhartha said.

"It's because you are a controlling and manipulative person. You think you have a proprietorship over my life." She hissed. "How are you different in your morale when you're doing the exact same thing to your girlfriend that I did back then to you?"

"It's not the same."

"How?"

"I loved you and you broke my heart, you kept me in the dark."

"And you think Aaradhya doesn't love you? She took you home to her mother. She tells her friends that you are the one. You're the one who doesn't revert. And so you cheat and think yourself to be unaccused. You're just ridding yourself of the guilt. But you're just as much of a criminal as I am."

The angle of diffraction depends upon the spacing as is evident by Bragg's Law. The properties related to the lattice depend upon the diffraction pattern.

I'd given up trying to follow the classroom pace of nanotechnology. By this time of the year, the only thing that was monstrous in my concerns was the career; and the future perspectives. I couldn't allow myself to cut the slack. I wanted Maa to stop working, I wanted to earn and study at the same time.

I sat, working on my phone under the desk, shortlisting the universities to which I wanted to apply. My list and majors had grown exhaustively long. Siddhartha sat near me, peering into my notebook, scribbling some sort of a calligraphic font absent-mindedly.

"You've been very detached lately." He said.

"I've been engaged, Siddhartha."

"I know. But I'm not asking for more than you can give. I'm not telling you to give me attention if you're facing time constraints. I'd only want to avail my relationship rights."

I slammed the notebook shut, exasperated and overworked.

"Siddhartha I don't know what the problem has been. I do feel I've been doing all that I can, yet somehow you think I am not enough."

Mrs. Mira Sharma was standing at the entrance of Dronacharya.

"Hello beta can you tell me where is room number 462?" She asked a passerby.

"Fourth floor, D wing." He said.

Mrs. Sharma walked around enquiring about Siddhartha's room and eventually, she found it locked. She fumbled through her purse, and pulled out her phone, her hands shaking.

"Hello Beta? Where are you?" She asked in a worried voice.

"Campus."

"I'm standing outside your room. Will you come?"

After some time, she saw Siddhartha walking towards her. His black t-shirt and Grey cargo reminded her of his husband's early looks. Siddhartha was a carbon copy of her husband, she couldn't help but notice the physical as well as mental similarity between the two.

He touched her feet without looking at her or embracing her. He unlocked the door and asked her to come in.

"It's quite an organized room, my dear." She noted. "You should keep the soap bars out of their case, else they dissolve in the waters in the corners of the case." She said, picking out the soap and putting it on a tissue paper on the slab to dry.

"Mom. Please. Don't touch my things." Siddhartha said irritated.

Mrs. Sharma turned around, her face soft and hurt. "If you say so."

Siddhartha had been so accustomed to living a hidden life, private and recluse that he despised even the slightest of interferences. He looked around the room worried that she might discover his canvases. He quickly shoved them under the bed with his foot.

"I was missing you terribly. I had to see you." Mrs. Sharma said.

"Mom, I can't do anything about your anxious thoughts," Siddhartha said grimly.

"You're just like your father. Same rotten blood" She said, and rose, storming out of the room.

"What the fuck Siddhartha?" I asked, my mind numbing itself. I had taken several minutes to register the fact that he'd been cheating on me. Had I not seen the evidence myself, I wouldn't have even believed any of it.

"Why?" I stood, shaking and crying.

"Why?" I repeated as he stood iced with silent selfishness.

"I can't keep doing this," I called Abhijeet crying. "Betrayal in the name of love. For what?"

"I know, please block him." He said.

I sat perched on the windowsill of my room, my legs dangling out, smoking cigarettes. Vanshika barged in, worried, "Get back in." She shouted.

I handed her the cigarette, she stood smoking while I told her everything.

"Why do you always have to wait and go through the worst? I always told you that you need to contain your emotions. You are always a blind believer Aaradhya."

I stubbed the cigarette and jumped back into the room, drawing the curtains.

"Well, it is what it is," I said, trying to pretend that I didn't care. I was great at denying my true feelings.

I am nothing like him. Siddhartha thought, staring at the eyeless face of the girl on his unfinished canvas. The rest of the painting along with the background had been meticulously drawn with great detail.

He wanted to live in a self-denial, awareness wrecked his head. How can my heart and art fail me?

He was filled with contempt. The sound of his dad's affair had dismantled his sense of home. It was one of the reasons for Sejal's death, yet somehow he had perpetuated the very grief that had crushed him not once but twice.

I am becoming what I hate. He thought horrified.

CHAPTER XXIX

Exoskeleton of a soft night

I scored decently on the GRE and IELTS. Applying for the universities was going to be my next step, I'd almost given up on wanting to pursue higher studies abroad, but the past two weeks had been terribly depressing. I'd find myself catching up onto the same old patterns- guilt, grief, insufficiency syndrome, body dysmorphia on repeat. I wanted to keep myself out of the loop and so, the doable thing was the only distraction that could make up for it.

Siddhartha had tried reaching me almost every day for the past two weeks, urging that I need to meet him to break up or I might really regret my decisions. I needed to hear him one last time and that he wasn't going to excuse himself for what he had done. Every text from him felt like some sort of a death note, like a battered elegy for the undead. I dreaded finding him on 'typing'.

Vanshika and Aakash would often shield me by being close (not that I needed assistance but it helped when I needed to be rescued from some panic attack).

Abhijeet had already bagged a placement in a core company and was grounded for partying with the other hostellers. Even though he insisted that I keep up with the social cultures, I found it threatening to leave the room until I really had to.

"I've marked your sixth proxy in a row, you can't keep shut in forever. Is that the kind of avoidance that you wanna live on?" Abhijeet asked.

"Thanks. I'll try to do better."

Kiran tried diffusing through a bunch of juniors to reach me. You've done the right thing, she conveyed. I was getting sick of the hypocrisy of the adult world. Never in my school had I ever been confounded with people who kept a double face and multiple personalities. I hated myself for trying to be good. All the moral policing that I subjected myself to seemed like a personal downfall lately. I found my head trapped in a string of how could you let this happen to yourself again. The 21st century Era of the genZs made me feel so out of place; cheating and dumping and playing cool was the only slang that made sense to the youth. I felt my exoskeleton, running low on ethical marrow. I was homesick for love, I needed somebody to mirror me and all that I got was disloyalty and shrewdness. Now the world could lecture me to focus on myself, you deserve better, yourself before else. But a broken heart only heeds to its internal cries.

Vanshika came into my room one night, looking tense.

"I've been shortlisted for another company but they want a data science kind of profile." She said.

"It's good that you applied, just focus on a bit of technical aspects and try to be as honest as possible," I said.

"Why don't you sit for placements too?" She suggested. "You got nothing to lose."

I agreed, and from the next week onwards, both of us applied to the same companies and luckily got placed in the same.

"Luck." I grinned.

"Congratulations Aaradhya," Siddhartha said, blocking the entrance of the class early one morning.

"Thanks," I said, trying to avoid looking at him, my heart catching a frenzy.

"Can we talk?"

"Ummm....." I looked around like I needed someone to answer for me.

"Please?" He pleaded.

"Okay"

"Can you come right now?"

Siddhartha and I sat on the stairs of the topmost hall of the lecture theater. I caught a whiff of the same citrus perfume that I'd once submerged into for comfort. It makes me nauseous now. It might be hers. I thought as I shirked away from him. He looked thinner than the last time I'd seen him, his eyebags swollen and dark. His knuckles were brazen with bluish-red bruises.

Great, he's been talking through his fists again. I thought, surrendering to a tiny sob. He tried to wrap his hand around my shoulder but I stopped him from doing so.

"I know whatever I did has no valid justification. I wouldn't even try to explain and argue. I just wanted to apologize." He said.

"How long has it been going?" I asked, biting my lower lip to stop myself from breaking into tears again.

"As long as I've known you."

"So you've been cheating on me for an entire year now? Congratulations on the anniversary." I said, venomous and pungent.

"Aaradhya, I really loved her and she cheated on me, I felt like my mother, small and unnecessary, powerless and detached. I didn't know how to get away from the person I'd placed so much faith in." He spoke.

"So you decided to shift me to the same place? Do you know how I feel? I feel invisible even to myself." I stammered.

Will you go to the fest with me? I promise I'll not try to have you back. Siddhartha texted.

Yeah.

The college fest, a three-day event was to be conducted in a week. Vanshika spent hours shopping and since Aakash was busy with some work, I filled his gap by being her female boyfriend.

I think you should go for that olive green bodycon. No, wine red is fine but it looks a bit gaudy. I'd suggest, and we'd spend the tired after hours, drinking lemonade and eating pizza.

"I like, peri peri over paneer tikka of the La Pinoz. Its bread is fine and so is the crust." I said, pulling apart a slice from a whole.

"What does it matter, you're always done in two," Vanshika said, sipping her Coke. "By the way you should buy that white slip dress, it looks so perfect on you."

"Yeah," I said absentmindedly, still thinking about my application for an education loan.

"You look a bit distracted, did he say something again?" Vanshika asked.

"Nope." I hadn't yet told anyone that I'd be attending the DJ night with Siddhartha.

On the DJ night, I stood waiting for Siddhartha, at our usual spot, feeling a little self-conscious. I'd cut my hair short and they were touching my almost bare shoulders in burgundy flame-like waves. The white dress was silky, almost slipped around my legs, and the thigh cut felt very revealing. I regretted wearing pencil heels, I regretted coming, I regretted my existence.

"Hey!" Siddhartha came closer and kissed my lips. I'd intended to turn away but couldn't. The softness of his lips sent a citric warmth in my veins. Bet, that's the taste of her lipstick. My brain concluded, hurriedly.

"Will you wait for me after the fest is over? I need to give you something." He said.

"Sure."

The disc lights bamboozled the harrowing night. The music poured out in waves. I gulped down another vodka shot, Siddhartha eyeing me with contemptuous disappointment.

"I've always hated alcoholics." He said. "My dad is one."

"Yeah." I'd started to loathe his dual nature, a fluctuation from right and wrong. His magnetic needles shifted faster than my anticipation could follow.

The swarm of bodies pressed and swayed around us, their skin glistening with sweat light of gothic-cyber-punkish hues.

I saw Abhimanyu pressed against his new girlfriend, he lifted her on his shoulders, while she smoked a joint.

A pang of disgust shuffled through my lungs.

"Let's change our place," I said, digging my nails into Siddhartha's arms.

"No, we won't." He glared.

When I tried to insist, he pulled me closer into a warm and comforting hug, "it's fine" He whispered.

The booze had started to have its transcending lightheaded effect. I yielded to his command, feeling ashamed and scared.

"What?" Vanshika said angrily. "You've been with Siddhartha?"

"Yeah, who else? I didn't wanna be third-wheeling you guys tonight. You deserve your privacy, after all, it's supposed to be the last fest of the college."

"Yeah, fair play. What about Abhijeet? You could've gone with him and his friends."

"I don't really know anyone else in his group." I tried to justify it weakly.

The glossy spring sun sparkled like a sequin in the sky bulging in an excessive exuberance. Winters were getting over, I thought happily. I hated winters, having to wear double-layered clothes and living inside the blankets in an elongated hibernation. The golden brown leaves rustled below my feet as I walked, falling along the pavements like freshly baked crepes and crusts. The skies shimmered shyly.

Three months to go, for the graduation to be over. I'd been counting the days on my fingers, my patience running out. The final year major project had been an extreme nuance, making me undergo an unnecessary penance.

CHAPTER XXX

Albatross

I last saw Siddhartha at our farewell party. Vanshika, donning an emerald green saree, flipping her straight black hair back, gestured in his direction. Siddhartha was standing at a buffet, holding Kiran's plate. The sight made me sick. He adjusted the strap of her golden blouse and she smiled. I suddenly remembered the scene of the Literary film screening, recalling having seen them making a fuss over something. It felt like a sharp deja vu.

I should've known. I thought, utterly embarrassed. Just as I turned around, Siddhartha called out my name. He was wearing a blue linen shirt with jet black blackberry pants and a Rolex watch, looking like some hot celebrity fresh out of the screen. I was dazzled by his brilliance, suffering from an inferiority complex myself. I looked down at my saree, coffee brown with white strands in a mehendi pattern. I hadn't been sure of the attire but Aakash and Vanshika had insisted that it suited my complexion.

"You look great." He commented as if hearing my thoughts.

"Thanks," I muttered.

"I just wanted to say that I still have the thing that I'd wanted to give you." He said, wrapping his arm around my bare waist.

"Well, you'd rather give it to Vanshika and I'll take it from her."

I wrapped up the final presentation of the final year, feeling greatly relieved. The social media accounts were spammed with, "Graduated Happily", "Made it out Alive", and "Survived". While all of these were true, I resonated with the last one the most. The last month had been so hectic and traumatizing that I'd started doubting my life. But now as I sat, with an acceptance letter from Caltech, my dream woven into a reality, I felt blissful. Though the voids that enter your emotional health are never filled or replaced, yet it felt better that I'd been a worthy daughter for my mother, and the thought brought me solace. I had taken Abhijeet out for a coffee, and we'd sworn to stay out of toxic relationships and prioritize our careers for a while.

Vanshika, Aakash, and I swept through the city, walking through the streets and our favorite eating places with a fondness and a reminder that we'd be doing it for the last time.

"I've been on a night out 4 times this month in the name of our last one," Vanshika said, blushing and out of breath, her hair frizzy and wet in the pre-summer heat. The temperatures soared, bringing back the memories of my school vacations. This is exactly how I'd feel back then, relaxed, reading extra books. I'd crammed my shelves with more novels in the past few weeks, buying like it was going to be my last day on earth very soon. I dived into a sea of explorations of how to live abroad, the cultures, the inclusiveness, crime hotspots, the best art museums, literary webinars, and research facilities. I tried my best to keep away from the perturbed emotions of my heartbreaks.

A few days before I was leaving for home, an unknown caller, identifying himself as a delivery person from Siddhartha Sharma called me. I went to collect the 'thing' that he'd been willing to give. It was a huge carton. After much panting and sweating, I dragged it into my room. The insides were double packages wrapped in newspapers. I sat, unwrapping all the layers. Canvases, his paintings.

I picked out the first, it read "Grunge dreams on a canvas": a perfect depiction of a sunset dripping into red emboldened wax across the blue skies, a scene probably captured from his hostel window. A dead raven, colored skies with pine trees, hillscapes: scenes from his town, a portrait of his mother smiling, his sister lying dead in the pool, his first kiss with Kiran, and the last one with an incomplete facial structure of some girl.

I stood, shaken. Why would he send such personal narratives to me? He had his own account and he'd never posted any of these. He didn't want these to be made public. What did he intend? What do I do with these snippets of his personal life? I fumbled through the corners and edges of the cartoon as well as the wooden frame of each and every canvas, searching for some note or clue. I dialed him and every time it ended with his phone being out of network. I called his friend, Vedanta who to my horror informed me that Siddhartha had been missing for 2 days now and he was unable to decide whether or not to call his parents.

"What do you mean he's missing?" I asked.

"He's not been in his room for the past two days and his phone is out of reach. He hasn't been online either and his last tweet was 3 days back, saying: the lasts are the firsts."

"When did you see him last?"

"Tuesday, night. In the mess. And to be honest he sounded fine and happy. I thought that maybe he was back with you."

I was reading the entire chats for the fifth time now, reliving all of our time together. I was particularly struck by, "You might regret this". And I really was. I felt like the mariner who killed the Albatross wantonly and spent the rest of his life and death, atoning for his sins, except in my case, I didn't seem to be able to find any conclusion or peace within. It had been a week since he went missing. The police authorities had been involved, his father had set out media and personal detectives. The authorities had questioned all of his friends and classmates about any clue related to him. I was however surprised that nobody had asked me anything so far. The highest possibility was being registered that he'd died by suicide someplace far off. I couldn't help thinking that it was all because of me and I could've saved him but I didn't because I was too busy distancing myself from the hurt of his disloyalty.

A few months later, I'm waiting at the airport, and I see a guy walking towards me, wearing a Rayban, holding Kafka's "The Trial". He looks somewhat familiar. He removes his glasses, his Russian-cut hair giving an immediate air of some faint recognition.

Siddhartha. I think. He looks in my direction, waves, and disappears.

Epilogue

Millions of years since the Big Bang eruption, millions since evolution, humanity has ceaselessly searched for an essence of living. As I embark on my late thirties, I have been dawned upon by a realization that no thought, art, or perception is honestly unique. There's no feeling that hasn't been felt before. The consciousness infiltrates like a tangible marrow through our congealed existence. Often when I write, I feel plagiarised by empathetic emotions. A writer or a lover can claim to boast uniqueness in their unmatchable words and promises of having discovered some things that no scientific discovery can analytically distill. Our bodies dance in a rhythmic amnesia of what our memories and experiences have trained us for. All coming-of-age stories share one thing in common- the belief that transitioning into adulthood and falling in love is a powerfully unique experience. It took me a couple of years to wipe out the tattooed blunders that left me aching for love, craving for a mirror to identify myself in. I had vowed to never venture out on the dumb-found absurdities of love. They felt like wires strangulated around my heart thundering the last bleeding palpitations. I deceived myself into an insurance against such assured blindness. I still think about Sid at the airport, his face etched as some blurred away the itch of a mysterious mystery. Abhimanyu has married twice since and is ensconced in a blissfully luxurious life. I would not shy away from saying how proud I am of his concerts and fame. I often hear his songs on repeat to recreate the fixture of a life that I am still amusingly trapped in. Siddhartha is still lost to me. I often have dreams about him. I wonder if the life that we once shared made any difference to his existence. When people lumber through eclipses of trauma and grief, they often show a concerning indulgence in behaviors that are hurtful to their mental health. He was rumored to be a victim of unlawful acts, clustered through a claustrophobic multitude of paranoid fits. All the attempts at rehabilitating his former artistic persona had been a failure. I had given up writing notes for him when all I received was an infinite restoration of silence, sticking like collateral of some unforeseen damage. His parcel still sits on my desk, unharmed and unappreciated. The abbreviated darkness that he buried like a sacred slumber often seeps and reveals itself into nightmares through my wakeful motions. Writing and Loving is not the same as loving writing or writing when in love. I would rest the nonchalant babble of my story here. It's not open to interpretation or up for a debated discretion. I would rather hide in shadows than reveal the true identities and lost meanings encapsulated in these bubble wraps of stringent emotions.

All these years count however stand the dilapidated state of lost friendships and falsely fostered acquaintances. Abhijeet and I were still in touch and his light-hearted accusations of me for being low-maintenance and unmarried were becoming terrifyingly irksome and mean.

"It's better than being trapped in an institutionalized bond of a loveless marriage," I said blatantly.

"Is that your excuse?" He guffawed. "No society is welcoming of opinions like yours. People who stay aloof allegedly reach the brink of insanity faster than others."

"Why? Do you think the quite some loneliness is far too unpardonable?"

"No Aaradhya. I just need you to see what I see." He crossed his arms around me, pulling me in a friendly gesture. "I see the motherly affection draining into an endless vacancy just because you're too naive to let go of your baggage from the past."

"I don't carry my past anymore."

"You wouldn't see the weight pulling you down. Is it not true that you are still gravitating into that traumatic abyss."

I looked at him, speechless. It's certainly impossible to entertain the harsh reality when you've been trying to falsely accuse yourself of being the calmest and the most peaceful version of yourself.

"You look like someone hoarding a tempest, ready to unleash the thunders on those who would care enough to listen.

All my life recurred in a repetition of trust being lost and found. But ten years later as I sit across the table, looking at him, I find myself wordlessly enraptured by the coincidence.

"How have you been?" He asks, his eyes burning with a soft twinkle.

"Good. I think."

"Family?"

"I live with my Mom." I chuckled.

"Wow."

After a long pause, he hands over a dusty Polaroid picture to me. I look at the old photograph grunge over time. I am smiling at the camera with a flourishing bougainvillea in the backdrop. I reminisce at the memory, surprised at how acutely I can recall every bit of conversation that we were having at the time.

"If you could beg for one constant in the world, what would it be?" I had asked.

"You just the way you are."

I smiled and he captured the moment. "Look how pretty this is." He'd beamed with pride. "I am always going to keep this on the wallpaper of every device that I will ever own." He had spoken. I just grinned in response, knowing that love-bound promises can be fickle sometimes.

"You are the reason I didn't act out on my impulses to give up on myself and engineering," Siddhartha spoke, bringing my attention back to the moment. "I felt burnt out and whimsical, cursing the stars that I was born under. I am not here to retrieve your love Aaru. I know

I have lost my chance. I just came here to apologize. I couldn't keep running away from what I did to you."

"It's alright Sid," I spoke, placing my hand over his. "I will never reach a conclusive state of affairs from the internal conflict that breaks my heart every day. I will never understand why the people who have suffered the most end up passing on the same fault-ended grief and live in denial."

"I can never repent enough Aaradhya. I am sorry for having corroded the binoculars of your worldview. I can only hope that one day you'll remove the spectacle and begin again for yourself."

I hand him his canvas paintings and he looks at me shocked.

"I am sorry Sid. I can't keep something that doesn't belong to me. Their weight is far too heavy for me to bear."

"I know." He picks up the carton and gets up. "I have never known what a happy home is like. I wish I wasn't burdened with a generational trauma that has snatched away my empathy to relate." He speaks, unable to meet my eye.

I hug him for one last time as we part ways, finally, attesting my belief to some cause-and-effect turn out of things.